GHOST TOWN

GHOST TOWN

by MICHAEL SLOAN

BearManor Media

2021

Ghost Town

© 2021 by Michael Sloan

Published in the United States of America by:

BearManor Media
1317 Edgewater Dr #110
Orlando FL 32804

bearmanormedia.com

Printed in the United States.

Typesetting and layout by John Teehan

ISBN—978-1-62933-696-1

1

Retribution

THE RIDER EMERGED out of the storm like a ghostly mirage. There was something otherworldly about him, as if he had been conjured up from the Gates of Hell. He bent in the fierce wind that buffeted him, the rainstorm eddying around him with malevolent force. He was seated precariously in the saddle with his hands holding onto the horn as the elements pummeled him. He wore a long gray duster with a black hat covering most of his face. A rifle in a scabbard was affixed on the saddle. It was difficult for him to make out the shapes of the deserted buildings in the gloom. The boardwalks were raised up at the saloon and the barber shop and the livery stable, but there was not a soul on them. The wind whipped around the streets creating little gusts of dirt eddying everywhere. The boulevards were a quagmire of mud with boards connecting them. The Rider passed an old, weathered sign that came into focus.

It said: *RETRIBUTION*.

It was a ghost town.

Rain lashed the dilapidated buildings on either side of the main street. The boardwalks were rotted and split.

Signs hung half-off their hinges or no longer existed. The rider saw a mercantile store, a town hall and a sheriff's office. All of them were deserted and echoed like ghosts wailing in the wind. The rider looked around and spotted three saloons, two hotels, a steakhouse and a tent city. Most of the tents were lying soaked across the sodden ground like silken shrouds.

The Rider dismounted in front of the Crystal Palace Saloon and tied his horse to the hitching post. He took a Winchester 94 rifle out of its scabbard and stepped up onto the boardwalk. Immediately his foot went through a rotted board. He freed it, drew a Colt .45 revolver from his holster and entered the saloon.

Tables and chairs were piled up in a corner. Dust covered everything. There was a long mahogany bar with a cracked mirror behind it with bottles still stacked under it. Stairs led up to a second floor with a balcony that circled the bar area. Cobwebs glowed in the corners. The Rider noted a poster above the gilt bar which advertised a vaudeville show. It featured *Eddie Foy for One Night Only* in a musical extravaganza where the entertainer was featured with long-legged dancers who were doing a cancan on the stage. The poster was torn as if one of the cowboys had tried to rip it off the wall.

The Rider listened to the silence. He thought for a moment that he had heard something from *outside* the saloon. But it was just one of the loose boards that creaked in the wind. The Rider holstered his Colt .45 revolver which had been a gift from Christopher Colt. He was not expecting company in Retribution---at least, not yet. He had about an hour to wait until there would be a sign of life.

The Rider picked up a chair and dropped it into the center of the room. He up-ended a round table beside it, then moved behind the bar. He found a bottle of Sam

Thompson rye whiskey. He uncorked it and tilted it down his throat.

Still drinkable.

He wiped the grime off a shot glass, sat down at the table and poured himself a shot.

Marshal Kyle Bascomb had just celebrated his forty-seventh birthday. He was a lean, brittle man with intelligence and compassion in his eyes. The town of Retribution was one he had ever wanted to visit again. He was there for one reason only.

Her name was *Skeeter*.

The Rider laid down the rifle on the table.

The drumming of the rain was magnified in the eerie silence. He took a swallow of the whiskey. He would hear them coming. They were not going to sneak up on him. They would come right through the doors of the Crystal Palace Saloon bold as brass.

He let his mind go back through the events that had brought him back to this *Ghost Town*.

It was the year 1892.

The town of Fargo Springs in the Arizona Territory lay near the town of Tombstone, circa 1882. A wedding reception was in progress. There were long tables piled high with food. Some fiddlers and guitarists were playing. The guests were boisterous and in high spirits. The beautiful bride, in her early twenties, was dancing with her groom, a handsome man, a little older than his new wife. At least fifty guests had gathered on the knoll of the hill outside the Spanish church. Children in pretty dresses and smart suits were running around having themselves a grand time.

Blackjack John Shackleton was smiling and clapping in time to the music. He was an intense outlaw with a ready smile but black, impenetrable eyes. He was in his late forties, looking constantly at the guests on the hillside for any sign of trouble. He was not expecting any but that was how he had lived for so long. His gang was spread out through the party, helping themselves to plates of food and wine.

A lean, scarecrow of a man, Paul Taggart, approached Shackleton with a plate of food. Taggart wore two guns on his hips. Blackjack thought Taggart had a psychopath's easy charm and baleful look.

"Much obliged," Shackleton said.

He took the proffered food. Taggart's gaze was constantly scanning the party and the forest surrounding the church. He acknowledged the bride and groom as they spun by.

He said: "Your sister sure looks beautiful, Blackjack."

Shackleton smiled. "Yeah. Wish her ma and pa were alive to see this day."

Taggart was amused. "They were your ma and pa, too."

Shackleton shrugged. "Ma got small and quietlike over the years till she rarely spoke a word to me. Pa beat me with that silver belt buckle until the night I wrapped it around his throat, then he gave me some room. But they doted on Beatrice."

As if on cue, the bride did a turn for Shackleton and Taggart.

Paul Taggart said: "Plague took them both, way I heard the story."

The newlyweds waltzed around past Shackleton. The outlaw leader smiled at both of them. "They would have died," the outlaw said, "if I had not put a bullet in their heads. Did not want either of them dying like that. Not even my old man." Shackleton suddenly laughed. "If that don't beat all!"

The groom had lifted Beatrice up onto a table where she was kicking up her heels to the delight of the guests.

In the trees around the copse of trees just outside the church and the picnic area, a large posse waited. Music played faintly from the wedding party through the thick trees. In the center the posse was the impressive figure of Marshal Jefferson Forrester, a big man, almost dwarfing his horse, a shock of gray hair going white at the temples. He was maybe sixty, with a florid face and a big handlebar moustache. Around him the members of the posse, all armed and carrying Winchester rifles, all with Deputy badges pinned to their lapels, were anxious.

Marshal Kyle Bascomb rode through the trees. He also had a Marshal's badge pinned on the front of his waistcoat. The posse parted for him to reach Marshal Jefferson Forrester. Forrester reined in his horse, which was skittish.

"Shackleton is there at the church and the picnic," Kyle told him.

Forrester let out a whoop of derision. "Dumb stupid bastard! Felt like he had to give his sister away because he blew their old man's head off. Good the way guilt can eat at ya. How many of his men are with him?"

"I counted twelve," Kyle said.

"Was Wendell Trask with him?"

"No."

"What about Paul Taggart?"

"He's there," Kyle said.

"Good enough," Forrester said, and wheeled his horse around.

Kyle grabbed his arm. "This is a *wedding* party, Marshal!"

"You think I give a good crap about that?" Forrester said. "I haven't ridden with a posse for eight days of eating dust and following false leads to let the bastard get away from me now."

"He can't go anywhere without our seeing him do it," Kyle argued. "Let his sister get married. Take him down once he leaves the church and the picnic area."

Forrester looked at Kyle, color rising in his face. "You feeling some kind of compassion for him, Marshal? Tell that to the Ellerston family! Oh, you cannot do that, can you? Because he murdered them all! Tell that to those three bank tellers that Shackleton gunned down outside of Tombstone. Tell that to Marshal John Elias who was shot in the back on an Abilene street."

One of the deputies, a mean-spirited deputy named Pete Talbert, rode up.

"There's a ten-thousand-dollar reward on Blackjack's head."

"You going to split that with posse, Talbert?" Kyle asked him, evenly.

Forrester wheeled his horse back around again. "This is about doing right and wrong, Marshal. We are in the right."

"There are women and children at the party," Kyle insisted. "Blackjack will get bored when the tequila runs dry and take his men out. We can hit them then."

"We'll hit them now when they ain't expecting us," Forrester said. "You got us this far, Kyle. Stay here if that is more to your stomach."

The marshal wrenched free of Kyle's grasp. Around him the deputies slid their Winchester rifles out of their scabbards. Forrester took charge.

"Go in hard and fast and shooting," Forrester said. "Do not let any of this scum get away. A thousand-dollar bounty for the man who puts Blackjack Shackleton in the ground."

On Forrester's signal, the posse rode through the trees. They left Kyle behind. For a moment he was torn. Then he rode after them.

Outside the church the festivities were in full swing. Blackjack Shackleton was still clapping to the music, standing at one of the buffet tables. But as he looked at the party guests a sense of foreboding came over him. He could not tell what had brought it on, but the fiddlers suddenly were out-of-sync in his mind. The ominous tone had swelled up in his head until it was overpowering. Into it the sound of galloping hooves came to the forefront. Shackleton turned around to see the members of Forrester's posse bearing down on the party guests.

Then everything went into slow-motion for him: The riders and their wild hollering and their horse's hooves kicking up the mud in front of the church. His gaze fell upon his sister Beatrice, smiling, radiant, but the smile had died on her face and her eyes widened in terror. The fiddlers and the guitar players had stopped playing, frozen in time.

All hell broke loose.

Paul Taggart drew both of his guns and starting firing.

There was instant pandemonium as the posse swept through trees, firing indiscriminately. Guests dove under tables and rushed for cover. Some of Shackleton's outlaws were cut down as they fired back at the deputies. Innocent guests were hit by the gunfire, spinning into each other, crumpling brokenly to the ground. Blood spurted in cascading showers.

Shackleton fired, running toward the bride, only to see her body riddled with bullets. More blood blossomed across her pristine white wedding dress as she fell to the ground. Shackleton let out a cry like a wounded animal.

On horseback, Marshal Jefferson Forrester fired at the outlaws. Shackleton took a bullet in the stomach. Paul Taggart galloped over to him and took Shackleton's outstretched hand. He heaved himself up on the horse behind Taggart. He looked around and saw Kyle Bascomb riding into the fray. Kyle fired, blowing one of Shackleton's outlaws off his horse.

Shackleton looked for a lingering moment at Kyle's face.

As if he would never forget it.

In front of Kyle, one of the deputies, caught up in the slaughter, killed a young man who was trying to protect the children. The deputy giggled, turning, finding another target, one of the bridesmaids. Kyle fired at him. The deputy lurched off his horse, sprawling into the dirt.

Marshal Jefferson Forrester's six-shooters blazed haphazardly into the crowd. His eyes were shining in his bloodlust. He gunned down two more of Blackjack Shackleton's outlaws, not caring that a young mother and her six-year-old son were trampled beneath the melee. Forrester caught Kyle's eye, but he was too far into the killing spree to care. He wheeled his horse around and charged through the rising dust cloud.

Six of Shackleton's gang, including Shackleton and Paul Taggart, rode through the chaos away from the church grounds. Most of the posse, led by Marshal Forrester, galloped after them. The rest dismounted, making sure the fallen outlaws were dead and trying to help the survivors.

Kyle dismounted. He had no intention of rejoining the posse. He grabbed a young girl before she could be trampled underfoot by a deputy's loose horse. Kyle set her down on the ground, shielding her. Around him the sound of the gunfire suddenly ceased.

All was deadly quiet.

The survivors picked themselves up from the ground. The groom lifted his bride's dead body into his arms, sobbing uncontrollably. Some of the deputies looked around them in horror: numbed, disoriented, as if none of them had expected this to happen.

Kyle fingered his Marshal's badge and unpinned it, but he did not throw it away. He pocketed it and moved over to where some of the other survivors were pulling themselves out of the dust.

In the *Ghost Town, 1892,* the silence in the Crystal Palace Saloon was palpable. The drumming of the rain on the boardwalks echoed incessantly. Marshal Kyle Bascomb sat alone at the upended table and poured himself another shot of whiskey. Little noises betrayed the stillness. The loose shutter still banged fitfully outside the Last Chase Saloon further down the boardwalk. Kyle thought he could hear horses approaching, but that might have been his imagination.

In Kyle's mind's eye he saw the Crystal Palace Saloon brighten as it had been in 1882, as if a new day had suddenly dawned. It brought with it the sounds of the town awakening. Sunlight reflected through the windows in front of Kyle Bascomb in a blaze of glory.

2

Skeeter

THE MAIN STREET of Retribution, Saratoga Street, was bustling with people and activity. Outside the Crystal Palace Saloon, a 12-year-old girl, dressed like a tomboy, walked down the boardwalk. She was a brunette with a pretty face and cornflower blue eyes with a rebellious look in them. Skeeter Shaw was fourteen and took the world by storm by sheer willpower. She noted a young boy, maybe a year older than her, jumping in and out of mud puddles, dodging around people.

A stagecoach suddenly careened through the mud of a recent rainstorm, the horses tired and erratic. On top of the stagecoach a heavyset man held the reins, Hoss Cavanaugh, a robust, bull-in-a-china shop kind of personality. Lettered on the side of the stagecoach was: *CAVANAUGH FREIGHT*. One of the townspeople waved a greeting to Hoss, who turned round. Hoss did not see the young boy who was running across the street trying to beat the horses to the other side.

Skeeter shouted a warning to him.

"Homer! Watch out!"

Hoss jerked on the reins, but the boy was going to be trampled underfoot.

A powerful pair of arms grabbed Homer Reneker and pulled him from beneath the horses' legs.

Skeeter plunged out into the street when she saw who Homer's benefactor was.

The gunfighter known as Doc Holliday dropped Homer unceremoniously onto the boardwalk. Doc was elegantly dressed, his hair long and slicked back. He wore a long black coat, black boots, a black string bowtie and a velvet waistcoat which had a gold watch chain attached to it. There was grace to his movements, but consumption had been eating away at his strength. He did not carry a gun, although the people in the street gave him a wide berth. He did carry an ornate silver walking cane.

Hoss Cavanaugh brought the stagecoach to a stop and climbed down. Homer was a freckled-faced kid with big green eyes. He was grinning at his near miss with death. Hoss grabbed him and shook him like a terrier shaking a rat, but his anger was triggered by fright that he had almost ran the kid down.

"Homer! Didn't you see me comin'? Those horses nearly trampled you to death!"

Doc said, mildly: "You aimin' to finish the job, Hoss?"

Hoss reluctantly let Homer go. Skeeter jumped up onto the boardwalk and put a steadying arm around Homer.

"You know Homer don't have a lick of sense!" she said to Hoss. She looked over at Doc Holliday with shining eyes. "You saved him, Doc."

"Purely a reflexive response on my part."

Hoss was clearly rattled. "I put you in a pine box, Homer, and your daddy comes lookin' to carve out my guts," he said.

"He wouldn't care," Homer said, carelessly.

Mayor Ballantyne, a big pompous weasel in a frock coat with a grandiose voice, strode down the boardwalk.

"What is the meaning of this altercation?" he demanded. "We have a dignitary of luminous proportions on the stage! This is no way to introduce her to our illustrious town." He grabbed Homer's face with mock concern. "You all right, son?"

Homer pulled away from his oily grasp. Hoss gripped Mayor Ballantyne's coat.

"Deke hears about this, I'm gonna know it came from your sleazy toad face, Mayor."

"I will ask you to unhand the senior official in this community," Mayor Ballantyne spluttered, "so that I may carry out my mayoral responsibilities."

Hoss dropped the mayor into a puddle. He scrambled up and scuttled around the stagecoach. Hoss started to unload the luggage. Doc moved on down the boardwalk, Skeeter and Homer falling into step beside him.

The door to the stagecoach opened and Mayor Ballantyne helped a beautiful brunette woman step out. She was in her early thirties with porcelain skin, dark brown eyes, exquisitely dressed. As she looked around Saratoga Street there as a hint of another life in her eyes, and in her demeanor. A sadness to her regal bearing that belied the remorse she was feeling. Hoss hauled down a steamer trunk that had stenciled on it: *MISSY VARTAN* and beneath that the words: *THE SONGBIRD OF EUROPE AND THE AMERICAS*. There was a colorful graphic design of Missy siting on a swing in a birdcage, an audience on their feet applauding all around her. Three members of her troupe, two courtly men and a beautiful brunette woman, stepped out of the stagecoach behind her.

Mayor Ballantyne was practically genuflecting in his haste to greet her. "Miss Vartan, I am Mayor Ezekiel Ballantyne. May I extend my profound apologies for the sudden stop to which you were just so rudely subjected and welcome you and your musicians with all the pomp and ceremony that one official can muster in the hot midday sun to the town of Retribution."

Missy looked around, as if she were seeing the town for the first time, a strange smile on her face. Mayor Ballantyne cleared his throat to get her full attention.

"The Pacific Hotel is the best we have to offer, where your suite is waiting with champagne and a sumptuous display of cheeses and pates. Once you are settled I will personally escort you to our Music Hall Theater, not as magnificent as the Bird Cage Theater in Tombstone, but equally commendable."

Missy nodded her head. "It's good to be home," she said, softly.

Mayor Ballantyne stopped in mid-gush, staring at her. "*Home*?"

"You may escort me to the hotel," Missy said graciously, and took his arm.

Major Ballantyne had been just transported to heaven.

On the boardwalk, Doc Holiday, Skeeter and Homer strolled along, passing the livery stable and the Last Chance Saloon.

Skeeter shoved Homer. "You might thank Mr. Holliday for hauling your sorry hide out from underneath those horse's hooves! What were you doin', you ragamuffin rat?"

Homer shrugged and grinned. "I figured I could get across the street before they stomped me to dust. I stumbled over a prairie dog hole."

Skeeter turned to Doc Holliday. "You sure were fast picking him up, Doc. It is okay that I call you Doc, right?"

"When I was a dentist my patients used the term loosely," he said, wryly.

"How come you don't carry a handgun?" Skeeter asked.

"You aimin' for me to shoot someone?"

"It is just for your protection! There is a rowdy element in this town who would be hankerin' to see you pull leather!"

"I am not a shootist," Doc said.

"Sure, you are!" Homer insisted.

"I'll bet you draw a handgun faster than you can blink an eye," Skeeter said, slyly.

Doc had not looked at either of them. "What gives you that idea?"

"Stories folks tell in town. Well, whisper more like. They say you are a notorious gunfighter. That you were with Wyatt Earp in Dodge City, Kansas and you saved him from a bunch of cowboys who were gonna shoot him in the back. That is true, ain't it?"

"Wyatt Earp is a careful fellow," Doc allowed. "He is unlikely to have let a bunch of cowboys get behind him."

"Then ya *do* know him!" Skeeter said, triumphantly.

"I believe our paths may have crossed once or twice. Don't believe every whisper you hear, Skeeter."

"Hey! You remember my name!" Skeeter said, beaming. "Sometimes I do not think you know I'm alive!"

"I seem to keep tripping over your feet wherever I go," Doc said, dryly.

Skeeter nodded. "My dad says that. He used to call me '*Scoot*'! He would say: 'Will you *Scoot*!' But I could not say the word '*Scoot*' when I was little, so I said: 'Skeeter' and so…" She shrugged. "Name kinda stuck. Tom Shaw is my dad. He is sheriff here in Retribution. But I am sure you already know that."

Homer suddenly said: "Does the sheriff have a wanted poster for you in his office?"

"There *was* an incident with a saloon keeper in Dallas some years ago," Doc said. "The man thought I was cheating at Faro. He did not understand I don't need to cheat those who have already cheated themselves."

"Did ya shoot him?" Skeeter asked, agog with excitement.

"I believe some shots were fired. I must have been in a generous mood that afternoon. I believe the man lived."

"Were you arrested?" Homer asked, his eyes like saucers.

"No charges were filed. But there could still be an old warrant on a sheriff's desk with an unflattering picture of me on it."

Skeeter suddenly looked concerned. "What if my dad calls you out?"

"I am confident that he won't do that," Doc said.

Homer turned breathlessly to Skeeter. "Doc would draw his pearl-handled Colt .45 with the quickness of a hummingbird's wing and your daddy would be looking at a hole in his chest."

Skeeter shoved him. "You take that back! My dad is fast!"

"When did you ever see him stroke leather?" Homer asked, dubiously. He turned back to Doc. "Mr. Reneker, he is my dad, he says that he ain't never seen Sheriff Tom Shaw ever pull his gun, even on a bar crawler at the Crystal Palace Saloon."

"Neither did Wyatt Earp when he was marshal of Dodge City," Doc allowed. "You can keep the peace without bloodshed if you are smart."

"You ever know a marshal smart like that?" Skeeter asked him. "Besides Mr. Earp?"

"There was one lawman who had some qualities I could admire."

"What was his name?"

"Kyle Bascomb," Doc said.

"Did he become your friend?"

"He was chasing me out of a town in the Dakotas called Silver Springs before a lynch mob could stretch my neck," Doc said, wryly. "We didn't get a chance to chat."

"How come you live on the edge of town in that broken-down old cottage?" Homer asked him.

"So folks will not bother me," Doc said, pointedly. "Or follow me around."

Suddenly Doc started to cough rackingly. He took a new handkerchief from his inside pocket and covered his mouth. He took out a silver flask and took a swig from it.

"That whiskey smells funny," Skeeter said.

"It is laced with laudanum," Doc said. "Purely medicinal."

Skeeter shook her head, suddenly very concerned. "You're sick, Doc. You should go and see a real doctor. Dr. Drake used to be the doctor here in Retribution."

"I believe he is residing in the cemetery. Might be difficult for me to obtain a diagnosis."

"But his widow is takin' care of the town," Skeeter said, quickly. "Her name's Rachel. You wouldn't mind a woman tendin' to ya, Doc, would ya?"

"She's got real soft hands," Homer said.

"How would you know?" Skeeter said, skeptically.

Homer just shrugged. Doc stepped off the boardwalk, stifling another agonizing cough with his handkerchief. Skeeter was troubled by Doc's condition, but she wanted to change the subject.

"You still got your pearl-handled gun, Doc?" she asked him. "I hear it's a beauty."

"Never did."

Doc took that moment to leave Skeeter and Homer behind. He was headed for the Crystal Palace Saloon.

Skeeter looked after him and smiled. "I like him!"

"You like everyone," Homer said.

"Do not!" Skeeter said, offended. "Don't like *you!*"

She strode off, but Homer followed, his grin returning.

Skeeter and Homer crossed over to the Pacific Hotel where Tom Shaw, Skeeter's father, stepped out. He was immaculately dressed, sporting a glittering Sheriff's badge, a gold pocket watch, a silk vest, a black frock coat, looking very much the part he most liked playing… a *lawman*. He was a tall, handsome, expansive man with a trimmed moustache and slick black, wavy hair. His voice had a well-modulated timbre that he used to great effect. Otis Larchmont, his deputy, mid-20's, dark, tousled hair, walked the boardwalk with him. Sheriff Shaw grabbed Skeeter and Homer from behind.

"If you are gonna skip school," he said, mildly. "do not walk bold as brass past the Longhorn restaurant of this hotel where you know I partake of breakfast every morning."

Skeeter gulped. Homer struggled in Shaw's grip, but that got him nowhere.

"Ain't no school today, Sheriff," he protested.

"Now there is an odd thing," Sheriff Shaw said. "You would think the schoolteacher, whom I happen to be married to, might mention to me that she had a day off to take the air and join me for a constitutional."

Skeeter kicked Homer's shin. "If you are gonna lie, Homer, make it a whopper and do it to the right person!"

Otis Larchmont grinned. "Reckon you can handle these outlaws on your own, Sheriff."

He moved away, crossing the street to the sheriff's office. Tom Shaw's mood was not so hearty now. "I am disappointed in you, Skeeter. You promised your ma you would stay in school."

Skeeter's voice was contrite. "I was going there right now, Pa. I am just late. Homer was nearly run down by Hoss Cavanaugh's stagecoach and I had to help him out."

"There is always some fanciful story that you are spinning, Skeeter!"

The Sheriff marched Skeeter and Homer down the boardwalk. They moved past a large second-floor balcony above the Crystal Palace Saloon. On the balcony Deke Reneker, a compact, ironic man, sat in a big cane chair, drinking coffee. He watched the people in Saratoga Street below him as if he owned it, which he virtually did. He was dressed in a silk suit, not quite as fancy as Sheriff Tom Shaw's apparel, but just as elegant. Behind him stood Jim Plank, a heavyset bartender who worked for Deke. He was already drinking whiskey. Below they noted the sheriff marching Skeeter and Homer right up to the white schoolhouse nestled between the telegraph office and the Last Chance Saloon.

Homer happened to be Deke Reneker's son.

The kids ran through the doorway into the schoolhouse.

Plank grinned. "Looks like your son is in trouble again, Mr. Reneker."

Deke took another swallow of coffee. "The criminal element in town must be dormant if the good Sheriff has nothing better to do than arrest children."

Plank shook his head. "Look at him strut! He just needs a few peacock feathers sticking out of his frock coat! Doesn't he know that no one in Retribution takes him seriously?"

"Our resolute and dedicated peacekeeper might surprise you one night," Deke said.

Plant belched. Deke sighed and looked the other way. He noted that Mayor Ballantyne had moved out of the Pacific Hotel with Missy Vartan, practically genuflecting his way toward the Music Hall Theater. That brought Deke Reneker to his feet.

"Missy!" he said softly.

Plank followed his gaze. "Yeah, Missy Vartan, right there in the flesh! She is quite the looker, ain't she? She is going to be playing tonight at the Music Hall Theater. Coming from her 'triumphant return to the St. Louis stage' or some horseshit like that."

"I know, Jim," Deke said, quietly. "I was the one who brought her to Retribution."

"I didn't know you had done that," Plank said.

"What you don't know about my life would fill many volumes of literature," Deke responded, acidly.

Outside on Saratoga Street, Mayor Ballantyne was pointing out the spots of interest to Missy Vartan, but his voice had faded into a blurred echo as Missy looked up at the backlit figure of Deke Reneker on his balcony at the Crystal Palace Saloon. He did not acknowledge her.

Inside the small schoolhouse, Alice Shaw, Tom Shaw's wife and Skeeter's mother, stood before a blackboard. There were twenty kids sitting at wooden desks, Skeeter and Homer among them. Alice had a chalk battlefield drawn on one part of the blackboard with the name *GETTYSBURG* above it and, on the other side, part of Lincoln's *GETTYSBURG ADDRESS.* Alice was a tall, willowy, fragile woman in her late 30's, with hands that fluttered like wounded birds.

"It was November in 1863 that President Lincoln rode down Baltimore Street to the Evergreen Cemetery in Gettysburg," Alice said, in a reverent voice that reverberated through the schoolhouse. "My dear friend from the east, Mrs. John T. Meyers, said his speech was very short. After it, there was no applause, only silence. Mr. Edward Everett had just given a two-hour oration before it, and…"

The doors to the schoolhouse burst open and Deke Reneker strode inside. The children's heads turned. Deke marched down the main aisle toward the place where Homer was sitting. Alice attempted to continue with her recital.

"Mr. Everett wrote the President a letter some weeks later saying: 'I should be glad if I could flatter myself that I came near to the central idea of the occasion, in two hours, as you did in two minutes'…"

Deke pulled Homer out of his seat by the ear. Alice stopped her history lesson, her tone severe, almost scolding: "Mr. Reneker! I appreciate the fact that you are Homer's father and therefore you have a voice in his education, but you are interrupting a history class!"

"Homer don't need to know about history," Deke said. "He needs to do his chores and help out at the Crystal Palace Saloon and make sure he doesn't get trampled by stagecoach horses." Reneker raised his voice for the benefit of the kids. "President Lincoln got careless. He would not allow a military presence to accompany him to social functions. He let down his guard and he was shot dead." Reneker turned back to their teacher. "That is the life lesson you should be teaching them, Mrs. Shaw."

Deke pushed Homer up the aisle and they both exited the schoolhouse. Alice looked distraught. The kids waited expectantly to see what she is going to do. She just threw up her hands.

"We will return to Gettysburg tomorrow," she said, her voice strained. "Class is dismissed for today."

The kids cleared out of the schoolhouse with a whoop and a holler, all except for Skeeter. Alice, almost savagely, erased everything on the blackboard.

"I thought we were gonna return to the battle tomorrow," Skeeter said.

"Why bother?" Alice said with savage intensity. "Once word spreads that Deke Reneker pulled his son out of school, there won't be a handful of children left here tomorrow. Their parents will follow Mr. Reneker's lead. He has got this town inside a closed fist."

"Not father, he don't," Skeeter said, defensively.

Alice's attitude softened a little. "No, not your father. But if he were called upon to confront Mr. Reneker, I fear what would happen. Thomas would bluster and pontificate, but he is not a man mindful of his surroundings. President Lincoln sat in a box at the Ford Theater in a rocking chair. The bullet from his assassin struck the back of his head. His assailant, Mr. John Wilkes Booth, was in the shadows behind him."

Tears suddenly filled Alice's eyes. Skeeter took her mother's hands to stop them from trembling.

"I will make sure no one will ever sneak up behind father," she said. "Do not cry, Ma. Deke Reneker is just a bully. All bullies step into the shadow of someone bigger one day."

Alice laughed through her tears, tousling Skeeter's hair. "My, you talk like you're already all grown up, Skeeter."

"Things are going get better for us here in Retribution, Ma. I got a friend in town now. Someone who will look after us. Only he doesn't know it yet."

"What on earth are you taking about, child? What friend is that?"

"You'll see." Skeeter pulled away from her mother's embrace. "I'd better go make sure that no-good Homer isn't getting himself into a poor state of mind."

Skeeter ran down the schoolhouse to the front door.

"Stay away from Mr. Reneker!" Alice said, plaintively.

"He don't scare me none," Skeeter said, and banged the door on her way out.

Alice sighed. "I reckon no one does," she said, softly.

3

General Store

WENDELL TRASK DISMOUNTED and tied his horse at the Retribution Mercantile and Grocery store. He was an outlaw who rode with Blackjack John Shackleton. He was tall, mean and deadly. He entered the mercantile store while Swede Norquist was serving Missy Vartan. Swede had a heavy Swedish accent and had lived in Retribution all his life. He was friendly and his manner unassuming. Mayor Ballantyne hovered fawningly near Missy Vartan. Doc Holliday waited at the grocery counter where he had purchased some canned goods, tobacco pouches and, incongruously, some small, thin paint brushes.

Immediately Trask reacted to seeing Doc Holiday. He knew a fellow gunfighter when he saw one. Doc had not seen him come in yet. Or it appeared that he had not.

"I will send everything over to your hotel, Miss Vartan," Swede was saying. "I'm going to throw in some lavender bath oil from Paris, France."

Mayor Ballantyne said haughtily: "I have already seen to Miss Vartan's bathing requirements."

Missy turned to him as if butter would not melt in her mouth. "Really, Mr. Mayor? Would they include at

23

least two of Deke Reneker's saloon girls? I do so hate to bathe alone."

Mayor Ballantyne gaped at her and sputtered, unsure of what to say. As if oblivious, Missy put a hand on Swede's shoulder.

"Lavender bath oil would be a delight," she said. "It is good to see you again, Swede. I wondered if you would still be running the mercantile store here in Retribution. I am told that Deke Reneker has bought up most of the merchant establishments in the town."

"Not mine!" Swede said proudly. "It will stay with me until the last breath in my body." He lowered his voice so only Missy Vartan could hear him. "I never thought I'd see you back in Retribution."

"That makes two of us," Missy murmured, but she did not elaborate. "Are you coming to the performance at the Music Hall Theater tonight, Swede?"

"I would not miss it for all the silver in the mother lode. Mrs. Norquist will be accompanying me, but she don't hear so good no more."

"She might find that a blessing." Missy said, wryly. Then she turned suddenly to Doc Holliday. "Will you be attending the performance tonight, sir?"

Doc shook his head. "No, ma'am. I am tone deaf."

Missy smiled. "That is too bad."

She moved toward the door, Mayor Ballantyne skittering across the floor to keep up with her. Swede went behind the counter to serve Doc. No one noticed Skeeter sneak into the store from the back. Wendell Trask stepped across the doorway and got into Mayor Ballantyne's face.

"How come you didn't ask me if I was going to attend your little songfest?"

"Perhaps because the smell of horse manure might deprive a diva of reaching several important notes,"

Mayor Ballantyne said, caustically. "If you'll step aside, sir."

Trask shoved the mayor back into some stacked cans, toppling them over. Missy remained cool and composed. "Do join us tonight," she said to Trask. "It is an opening night. They are always the best."

"Or you and I could go to your hotel room," Trask suggested, "and drop some of that lavender bath oil into your tub and get acquainted before the concert?" He leaned close to Missy. "I reckon I could show you a hell of a lot better time than three of Deke Reneker's whores."

"I doubt it," Missy said. "But I will keep that in mind."

Trask gripped her arm. "Maybe I will insist," he said.

Doc pulled Trask off Missy. Trask spun around, going for his gun, then saw that Doc was unarmed.

Doc said: "Time to escort the lady back to her hotel, Mr. Mayor."

Mayor Ballantyne preened as if *he* was the one coming to Missy Vartan's rescue. "Allow me to escort you outside, Miss Vartan."

Under the counter, Skeeter watched all this with wide-eyed excitement.

Missy turned to Doc. "What's going to happen when I leave?"

"Nothing at all, ma'am," Doc promised her.

Missy smiled and nodded her approval. "You're very gallant, sir."

Mayor Ballantyne was already out the door. Missy Vartan followed him. Swede had surreptitiously taken a shotgun from beneath the counter and laid it down beside Doc's canned goods. Trask was still looking at Doc with murderous intent.

"I know who you are, Doc," he said.

"Is that a fact? I thought my reputation had suffered from neglect."

"I see you ain't carrying a gun. Did you hang it up by the fire along with your backbone?"

Doc appeared to consider that. "Perhaps that is where I left it. Thank you for that insight."

Doc turned away. Trask backhanded him, sending him into the counter. A trickle of blood seeped from his nose. Doc's hands bunched into fists. From her hiding place under the counter, Skeeter mouthed: "Fight him, Doc!"

Doc unclenched his hands and turned back to the counter. "What do I owe you for the groceries, Swede?" he asked.

"I put it on the tab," Swede said, his eyes never leaving Trask's face. "You pay me another time. I deliver your goods to your cottage before evening."

Trask had not finished with Doc yet. "Go home and get that pearl-handled Colt .45 I heard so much about, Doc. I will meet you out in the street."

"I have nothing to fight you about," Doc said.

"How about the lady's honor?"

"I would say she can look after that herself. I am not looking for any trouble, although it does appear to seek me out on occasion."

"You're a coward," Trask said.

Swede picked up the shotgun and slammed it into Trask's belly. He drew his gun very fast, then his hand froze as he looked down at both barrels.

"You going not to be much of a fighter with your balls and legs on the other side of this counter," Swede said.

Slowly Trask holstered his gun. Doc moved to the door. Trask gave him a contemptuous look. As Doc exited the general store, Trask turned back to Swede.

"Stand down. I just came in for supplies. Got the list right here. I will apologize to the lady."

Swede took the list but kept the shotgun on the counter. Skeeter streaked out the door after Doc. Trask was startled.

"What the hell was *that*?" he asked.

Skeeter raced out into the streets. Clouds had obscured the sun. It was almost dark out. Distant thunder rolled. The storm was pretty far away, but the atmosphere was oppressive. Skeeter caught up with Doc on the boardwalk, almost tripping him. Doc just shook his head.

"You again?"

"I was in the mercantile," Skeeter told him, breathlessly. "Pretty smart move you made in there."

"I did not make any move at all," Doc said.

"Sure, you did. You got the singer lady out the door with no trouble and you let that big ugly fellah step in the shit." Doc looked at her. "Language. Sorry. Ma says it don't come seemly from the mouth of an angel. But I ain't one, so I guess that is okay."

"It is not okay with me," Doc murmured.

Skeeter nodded. "I'll chew down on it. You better get your gun, though, Doc. Pearl-handled or not, you wanna be ready if that big fellah calls you out."

"He won't. Stop getting under my feet, Skeeter."

They turned the corner of Saratoga Street. Doc Holliday had a small, modest cottage nestled under some oak and flowering cherry trees. He stepped onto the front porch. Skeeter ran up behind him.

"Can I come in?" she said, still out of breath.

"No," Doc said, shortly.

He opened the door. Skeeter held back, a little awed that she was on the threshold of Doc's house. She said: "Promise me you'll keep in the moonlight when you are out takin' a constitutional. Watch the shadows. Some elements in town would like nothing better than to notch their guns at the expense of your hide."

"I will give it some thought," Doc allowed.

Skeeter smiled. "See you later, Gunfighter."

Doc turned back to her. "I am a gambler. I am not a..."

But Skeeter had run off. He sighed, shaking his head. "You are my huckleberry."

Doc entered his cottage and shut the door behind him.

Inside his small, cramped office just off Saratoga Street, Hoss Cavanaugh sat at a desk, small, pinch-nez glasses perched on his nose, incongruous to his size. He was pouring over a blueprint of what looked like an armored vehicle. It was a stagecoach that had been mounted with armor panels with slits for rifle barrels. Above the graphic were the words: "*IRON MAIDEN*". Wendell Trask entered the office and moved up to Hoss's desk.

"Pretty fancy-looking stagecoach," he remarked.

Hoss quickly turned the blueprint over. "Ain't for passengers," he said, shortly. "What can I do for you, mister?"

"Got some freight I need haulin' to Fargo Springs," Trask said. "Personal belongings. When is your next run there?"

"Friday," Hoss said. "That's if the storm don't hit too hard. Last time the bridge washed away. What you got your belongings packed in?"

"Four crates," Trask said. "I wanna go with 'em. You need a gunhand?"

"Not on that run." Hoss squinted at Trask in the gloom of his office. "I know you, don't I?"

Trask extended his hand. "Wendell Trask. Working as a Faro dealer at the Last Chance Saloon."

Hoss shook his hand, getting back to work. "Reckon I mistook you for someone else. Nice to meet you. I got to get back to work."

"See you Friday, Hoss," Trask said.

He exited the office. Hoss looked after him suspiciously, then turned the blueprint of the Iron Maiden back over and examined it.

Dr. Rachel Drake's house was on the outskirts of Retribution, just below the church and cemetery. A brass plaque affixed to her front door read: *DR. SAMUEL DRAKE.* Inside, the house was nicely furnished. A big room served as an examination room for Rachel's patients. At the end there were two small bedrooms and a lounge where a claw-tub sat. Curtains were drawn at the windows, making the room dark. Water glistered in the tub. Rachel moved through the overlapping shadows wearing a thin wrap to the tub. She was a beautiful redhead, in her thirties, volatile and down to earth. She dropped the wrap, stepped naked into the tub and sank down into the hot water with a sigh.

A gun barrel came to rest at her head.

The hammer clicked back.

Rachel froze. Paul Taggart, one of the outlaws who had been at the bloodbath at the church with Blackjack Shackleton, knelt beside the tub. Both of their voices were hushed in the gloom.

"Where's Doctor Drake?" he asked.

"I *am* Dr. Drake," Rachel said.

"You're the Doc's wife."

"My husband was killed in a gunfight two years ago in town. I took over his practice."

"I never heard of a woman doctor before," Taggart said.

Rachel was not afraid of Taggart, although she knew she had reason to be. She recognized him as one of the outlaws that rode in Blackjack Shackleton's gang. Her husband had treated him for a passed kidney stone two years before. Her manner was not brusque, but authoritative.

"I trained at a hospital in Philadelphia," Rachel said. "I came here with no intention of being anything but a wife. But when my husband died it left the town without a physician. What do you want?"

"I got a man badly gut shot," Trask said. "I need to bring him here."

"Take the gun away from my head," Rachel said, "and I'll consider it."

Taggart moved the gun from Rachel's temple, but he did not holster it. "He's got a reputation."

"You mean he's wanted by the authorities?" Rachel said.

"He is. That change your mind?"

"I treat the sick. I do not judge them."

"Your sheriff wouldn't take kindly to my boss being treated," Taggart said.

"Sheriff Shaw knows how to stay out of harm's way," Rachel said, her voice ironic. "But I don't treat patients at gunpoint."

Taggart holstered the gun and straightened. He glanced down at Rachel's magnificent body. She tensed, but if Taggart had any reaction he kept it to himself.

"We'll be here after nightfall," he told her. "If there was anyone waiting for us but you…"

"There won't be," she said.

Taggart nodded, as if he understood. "Hippocratic Oath, ain't that what it's called?"

"That's right," Rachel said, levelly. "Now, if you do not mind, the water in this bathtub is getting cold."

Taggart did not leave her yet. "Must be tough," he said. "Townsfolk can't really put their trust in a female doctor. But when they are sick, they will expect you to treat 'em as soon as you can. If you let them die, you would be run out of town."

"Are you done looking at my breasts, or do you have something else in mind?" Rachel asked him.

He shook his head. "Not a thing, Doctor."

He moved toward the door.

"What's the name of your boss?" Rachel asked.

He turned back. "Blackjack John Shackleton." She gave a start of recognition. Taggart nodded. "Most folks in these parts have heard of him. He got shot defending his sister at her wedding. A posse cut her down like a dog in the street. You can pin a Marshal's badge on your coat, but that don't make you right. Some members of that posse, it just made them mean. I will be back directly. Do not tell anyone about this conversation. It is our secret. Understand?"

Rachel nodded. Taggart disappeared into the shadows of the room. Rachel let out her breath very slowly.

Kyle Bascomb rode into the town of Fargo Springs. It was bigger than Retribution, fancier facades on the buildings, many more side streets. Kyle tethered his horse to the pitching post and entered the Fargo Springs Saloon. It was crowded, the ambience boisterous. A piano player was pounding out a number in a corner. Kyle moved up to the bar. He signaled for a bottle of whiskey. The bartender poured a glass for him. He had noted the Marshal's badge on Kyle's vest.

"I heard it was a turkey shoot at that wedding outside Tombstone," he said. "You got most of the bastards, didn't ya?" Kyle did not answer. "Too bad Blackjack Shackleton turned tail and ran," the bartender said. "You goin' out after him again, Marshal?"

"No call for me to do that," Kyle said. "Jefferson Forrester has all the men he needs."

"He has been calling for volunteers to make up the new posse. He's here in town."

Kyle assimilated that information, then poured himself a second shot and downed it. The bartender went away. A poker game was going on at a table in the center of the saloon. Kyle picked up the bottle and moved to the table. The dealer was a laconic man, dressed in black, with a fancy waistcoat and a pocket fob watch on a silken chain. He had bright, intelligent eyes and a trimmed moustache.

This was the legendary Wyatt Earp.

His eyes flickered over to Kyle as he sat at the poker game, noting the Marshal's badge on his vest. Kyle tossed money onto the table. "This a friendly game, gents?"

"That may depend on much you want to lose," Wyatt Earp said, wryly.

"You look like a tolerable bunch. I reckon I will sit in."

Wyatt dealt the cards to the players at the table. "What brings you to Fargo Springs. Marshal?"

"Blackjack Shackleton," he said. "Jefferson Forrester put together a posse of deadbeats and the scum of the earth to apprehend him. I was part it. Forrester and I have some unfinished business. I heard he came here to Fargo Springs."

"I haven't seen him," Wyatt said. "What are you fixin' to do if you do find him?"

"Ain't decided," Kyle said. "You got a problem with that, Marshal?"

"I am not a marshal anymore," Wyatt said, affably. "I am just here to deal cards."

Wyatt dealt the cards. Kyle said: "I hear you are good friends with Doc Holliday."

Unconsciously, Wyatt Earp echoed Doc. "I believe our paths have crossed once or twice. I hear he settled down in some town east of here. Name of *Retribution*."

"I can't rightly say," Kyle responded.

Wyatt Earp dealt another hand to the players at the table.

Sometime later Kyle was on his third bottle of rye whiskey. His mood was dangerous. One of the deputies from the massacre at the wedding, Pete Talbert, slid into a table near the bar. He was watching Kyle at the poker table, sizing up his physical and emotional condition. One of the cowboys won the next hand. Kyle threw in his cards. He was down to his last few dollars.

Wyatt Earp said: "Better leave yourself enough for a room and some comfort."

One of the saloon girls, Lilly, sweet-faced with strawberry blonde hair, came over to the table. Kyle picked up the last of his money and walked unsteadily from the table. He allowed Lilly to put an arm around him as they headed for the stairs.

"Don't have enough money," Kyle murmured.

Wyatt signaled to the saloon girl. "Lilly, put your time on my tab."

She nodded and helped Kyle up the stairs to the second floor. Wyatt dealt another round of poker. Behind him in the saloon, Pete Talbert finished his whiskey and made his way through the swing doors out onto the boardwalk.

Marshal Jefferson Forrester stood on a second-floor balcony of the rooming house across the street from the Fargo Springs Saloon. He got a signal down on the street from Talbert telling him that Kyle Bascomb was in the saloon.

That was all the information that Jefferson Forrester needed.

4

Wyatt Earp

LILLY MANHANDLED KYLE to one of the upstairs rooms. It was opulently furnished with a wrought-iron balcony above the street below. Kyle and Lilly wrapped their arms around each other as soon as they collapsed on the bed. Their clothes fell onto the floor as they embraced, naked and sweating, but it was Kyle who was the one who was passionate and vulnerable.

Some time later moonlight streamed in from the open balcony door into the bedroom suite. Lilly's figure was sleeping fitfully, wrapped up in the covers. Kyle lay beside her, fully dressed, bathed in perspiration, his breathing shallow. He was sober now. His gun belt lay across the room on a chair.

He had come to a decision. He would turn his Marshal's badge over to the sheriff in St. Louis. Before that could happen, though, there was someone he needed to see again. Someone who had stirred his dreams. He had been in love with Rachel Drake for a long time, but the timing had never been right. He had left it too late to contact her. Maybe two years. He shook his head in the darkness. Had it been that long? But he had a longing to see her again. Rachel would either take him back in her arms or she would reject him. He thought the latter was likely to happen, but now he did not have anything to lose.

First he had a score to settle with Marshal Jefferson Forrester.

Kyle heard a small sound. It had come from the balcony outside the room. There was no time to reach for his gun. He slid off the bed, stuffed a pillow under the covers and stepped back into the shadows.

Pete Talbert came in fast from the second-floor balcony, gun in hand. He pumped two bullets into Kyle's pillow under the covers. Lilly awakened and started screaming. Kyle tackled Talbert from out of the shadows, hurling him to one side, then dove for the chair. Talbert got off one shot, then Kyle had his gun out of its holster and fired. Talbert got through the doorway before a piece of it splintered off. Kyle moved toward a terrified Lilly.

"You all right?

She nodded, clutching the covers around her naked body. Kyle ran through the doorway out of the room.

Talbert was almost at the bottom of the wooden staircase leading into the saloon. The saloon was seemingly deserted. No patrons, no piano player, no bartender. Talbert disappeared into the darkness below.

Kyle moved down the staircase.

Wyatt Earp sat at a back table, in deep shadow, playing solitaire. There was no one else around him. Talbert knelt down beside a table. Wyatt's gaze shifted. Two more of the deputies from the wedding slaughter moved among the tables. They did not see Wyatt.

Kyle turned the corner of the stairs.

Talbert raised his voice. "You shot my friend in the back, Marshal. At the church."

"He had it comin," Kyle said as he descended further down the stairs.

"Are you handin' out justice now?" Talbert sneered. "Thought you swore an oath to uphold the law."

"There was no justice at that wedding," Kyle said. "No lawmen. Just killers with a bloodlust. I know. I was one of them. I am coming for Jefferson Forrester. Send him that message."

"I already made him aware that you were in Fargo Spings," Talbert said. "He is expecting you."

Talbert was luring Kyle toward him. The other two deputies had a clear shot at Kyle as he cleared the stairs.

Wyatt stood up. He drew his Colt Buntline Revolver with its 12-inch barrel and fired in one fluid movement. One of the deputies sprawled to the floor. Wyatt cold-cocked the second deputy with the barrel of his gun. Talbert whirled to where he thought Kyle was.

He was no longer there.

Kyle fired his Colt .45 revolver from the shadows at Talbert. Talbert collapsed onto the floor. Kyle looked over to where Wyatt Earp was standing.

"Much obliged, Marshal," he said.

"I already told you, I am not a marshal anymore," Wyatt Earp said. "You had better get out of here before that posse comes back looking for the stragglers."

Kyle nodded. "Make sure Lilly doesn't suffer for taking me into her bed."

"I'll look out for her. Where will you go now?"

"There is someone I need to look up. In that town of Retribution you mentioned."

"Do you know Doc Holliday?"

"We are acquainted."

"If you happen to see Doc in Retribution, you could tell him I'm on my way back to Tombstone."

"I'll do that."

Kyle did not move for a long moment.

"Pete Talbert worked for Jefferson Forrester," Wyatt said. "I figured Forrester heard you were in Fargo Springs and sent Talbert to your hotel room to do his dirty work. That was the way Forrester worked. There will be another hired gun to take his place."

"Where might I find Jefferson Forrester?" Kyle asked.

"Over at the Bull's Head Saloon across the street. He has a suite of permanent rooms on the second floor. Or you can untether your horse and ride on."

"What would you do?"

"It don't matter what I would or not do, but I reckon you need to set the matter right."

"Would you be comin' with me?"

"I would not," Wyatt said. "This is your affair. Handle it the way it suits you."

Kyle nodded. "Much obliged again, Marshal."

Kyle moved through the saloon doors and out into the stormy street. Rain had started to pelt down, bringing visibility down to just a few feet. Kyle crossed the main thoroughfare. The Bull's Head Saloon was on the corner beside an alleyway. Kyle looked inside. There were a few cowboys at the tables and one Faro dealer who was looking for a game. Kyle climbed the wooden staircase to the second floor and found a sliding glass door. He opened it. A low-lit corridor led off into darkness. He moved down the corridor, thinking he would have to break down every door when he heard a woman's scream. It came from the last room on the left.

She sounded terrified.

Kyle tried the door. It was locked. He took a step back, brought his leg up and kicked at the flimsy lock. It shattered. Kyle followed it into the suite of rooms.

The lamps were all turned down. There were two of the saloon girls in the room, both of them naked, both of them cringing back from Jefferson Forrester's wrath. The brunette, Kyle put her age around twenty, was bleeding from a split lip and lacerations to her face. Beside her was a blonde saloon girl who was even younger, more defiant, but she had a black eye and it looked as if her face had caved in from the beatings. Jefferson Forester towered over them, naked, and with his own bloodlust consuming him. Kyle had no doubt that for whatever reason he was going to beat these two saloon girls to death.

Forrester whirled in the bed, spittle forming on his mouth, enraged at this intrusion of his privacy. His eyes opened wider when the recognized the marshal who stood before him.

Forrester pounced onto a Colt .45 revolver beside the bedsheets.

Kyle drew his .45 revolver and blew Forrester away.

The saloon girls scrambled off the bed. One of them, the blonde, ran immediately from the room. The brunette caught Kyle's arm.

"That was Jefferson Forrester you just gunned down," she said, her left eye almost closed. "He was scum, but he was well-liked in this town. You best ride on while you can."

"I aim to," Kyle said. Gently he touched the girl's abrasions. "You're all right?"

She looked at him with shining eyes. "I am now."

"What is your name?"

"Jessica."

"Have your doctor tend to those abrasions on your face. They will heal."

She looked down at the naked body of Jefferson Forrester on the bed. Kyle put a wrap around her shoulders. "Go downstairs."

Jessica nodded her thanks and retreated from the room. Kyle looked down at Jefferson Forrester. The sheriff in Fargo Springs might issue a warrant for Kyle's arrest. On the other hand, Kyle thought that Wyatt Earp might have a say in that.

But Kyle was not going to linger is Silver Springs to find out.

He closed the door to the suite, climbed down the wooden staircase and found his horse tethered to a hitching post. He thought for a moment that he saw Wyatt Earp's shadow outside the Fargo Springs Saloon, but he could not swear to it. He rode into the rainstorm that still churned the streets to mud and was lost to sight.

Wyatt Earp went back inside the Fargo Springs Saloon. He sat down at his table. He resumed his Solitaire game as if three men did not lie dead at his feet and a fourth one was lying in one of the rooms in the Bull Head's Saloon across the street.

Two days later, in the town of Retribution, Sheriff Tom Shaw stood in front of a mirror, pouring some cologne over his hands. He looked elegant and darkly handsome, wearing the Sheriff's badge on the lapel of his coat. Alice entered the bedroom and picked up an evening gown from the bed. She and her husband were going to the musical show at the town hall that night. Alice was still seething about what happened in the schoolhouse with Deke Reneker.

"Mr. Reneker dragged Homer out of school two days ago. Our daughter thinks her best friend is a gunfighter. I cannot live in this place any longer, Thomas. I want to go home."

Shaw turned to face her, catching a glimpse of himself in the mirror to make sure his moustache was well trimmed. "Alice this is our home." he reminded her.

"No! We followed you here to start a new life. It is a sham. There is no sophistication, no wit, no social conscience in Retribution. It is uncouth and undisciplined."

Shaw had weathered Alice's depressions before. "We're going to the Music Hall tonight! Just pretend you are back in Philadelphia and…"

"I don't want to pretend," Alice said, her frustration building. "I want to *be* there!" She gripped Tom Shaw's hands. "We need to leave this place, Thomas! Today! Just take what we would need for the journey. Hoss Cavanaugh could ship our things to us."

"I am the sheriff in Retribution, Alice," Shaw said patiently. "People count on me. I cannot leave them to the unlawful and the ungodly."

"You are a joke in this town," she hissed at him. "Everyone knows you'll never draw that beautifully polished gun from its well-oiled holster. It is just something you put on in the morning to look good when you strut around being important and needed."

She blushed at her tirade and turned away from him. The sheriff stood awkwardly for a moment, then he went back to the mirror and trimmed a little more off his moustache.

"We are staying here in Retribution," he told her, tersely. "This is not a conversation we'll have again, Mrs. Shaw."

Skeeter, in a party dress, had moved to the open doorway. In the mirror she could see her mother crying soundless sobs. If Shaw saw this, he chose to ignore it.

Inside the apartments on the second floor of the Crystal Palace Saloon, Deke Reneker was dressed in a red silk suit, black vest and coat, and polished boots. He loaded a small derringer which he put into a concealed slot in the sleeve of his coat along the forearm.

Missy's voice said: "A snake's kiss. That is what you always said the derringer was."

Deke turned. Missy Vartan stood in the doorway of the room. Faintly, Deke could hear the sounds of the raucous saloon below. Missy closed the door.

"I didn't think I'd see you face to face until after the concert with the whole town watching," Deke said, as if impressed.

"There were many concerts held here as I remember. I was very young when I left Retribution."

"And look at you now!" Deke said. "The 'Songbird of Europe and the Americas'. It suits you. You look confident, Missy. Radiant."

She walked up to him and slapped his face. It barely rocked him.

"That's for never writing to me."

"I didn't believe you would want to hear from a lowly saloon owner and whoremonger," he said.

"I used to be so frightened of you," she said, softly.

"But now you're a different person," Deke said.

"No, I'm the same young woman you taught to be a saloon girl from the age of twelve. I just look at the world differently now."

"And how do you see me through these new and challenging eyes?"

"You're still the same arrogant, self-serving reptile you always were," Missy said.

Deke took a step back from her. "You could have made that judgement from across a packed music hall auditorium."

"I wasn't certain you'd be attending the concert," Missy said.

Deke shook his head, as if saddened by her attitude. "I wouldn't miss your opening night for anything in the world."

"Is Homer coming too?"

"He's not too comfortable in his store-bought Sunday suit," Deke said. "But he'll be there. It is good to see you again, Missy. It warms my heart."

"You don't have a heart," Missy said.

"Then it warms my balls," he said.

A small smile touched Missy's lips. "That I believe."

Deke's voice took on a kinder lilt. "What is it you came to say to me?"

"I don't rightly know," she confessed.

Then she turned on her heel and left the room. Deke gazed after her with what almost looked like pain in his eyes.

An hour later, elegantly dressed people were streaming into the Musical Hall Theater in Retribution. A banner had been strung across the entrance that said: "*MISSY VARTAN -- OPENING NIGHT*". Mayor Ballantyne was at the doors to the theater greeting everyone, ushering them inside. Deke Reneker was there with Homer, who was dressed in an uncomfortable suit, pulling at the collar of his shirt. Tom Shaw was in the crowd greeting friends and acquaintances. Beside him, Alice was radiant in an evening gown. Skeeter had on her yellow dress. She and Homer exchanged comradely horror at the sight of each other's outfits. Swede and his wife, a pale, Swedish woman named Hannah, were shaking hands with friends.

Outside of town, a storm was gathering. Thunder rolled ominously. A buckboard pulled up to the side of the Drake house. Paul Taggart and another outlaw, a lanky and muscular man, Curly Bob Thornton, threw back a tarpaulin and pulled the wounded Blackjack John Shackleton out. He was barely conscious. Another outlaw, Jake Turnbull, a big man with a bushy beard and a soft voice, waited outside. Taggart and Curly Bob carried Shackleton around to the front. Taggart knocked on the front door. Rachel opened it and they moved inside. Taggart and Curly Bob laid Shackleton down on a wooden table illuminated by two strong lamps. Shackleton was ashen, bathed in perspiration. The bottom of his shirt was covered in blood, some of it fresh. Curly Bob looked around the front room of the house.

"Who else is here?" he asked.

"No one."

"You live alone in this cottage?"

"Since the death of my husband."

"You have no objection if I looked around some?"

"I can't stop you."

Curly Bob moved away to search the house. Rachel handed Taggart a pair of large scissors. "Cut off his shirt," she told him. "Try not to move him if you can help it."

Taggart did as he was told. Curly Bob returned, holstering his gun. "Nobody here."

Taggart pulled Shackleton's shirt off. Rachel examined the bullet wound with gentle, probing fingers. Shackleton moaned, drifting in and out of consciousness.

"The bullet's in deep," Rachel said. "I got a scalpel sterilizing in boiling water."

"Are you planning on digging the bullet out of him?" Taggart asked.

"Unless you've got a better idea?"

"No, ma'am," the outlaw said. "We'll give you a little space."

He stepped back from the table. Rachel looked down at Blackjack John Shackleton's face, knowing it was rumored that he or one of his gang had killed her husband Samuel. It gave her a moment's pause. If her hand slipped on the scalpel, none of the outlaws would hold her responsible. She owed them nothing. But she was a physician and healing the wounded was part of her calling.

She went to work on Shackleton's injuries.

In retribution, Wendell Trask sat in the Cristal Palace Saloon drinking whiskey. The other outlaw members had left to go to Dr. Rachel's house with Blackjack Shackleton in the back of a buckboard. There was nothing more for Trask to do, except say a prayer for his boss. He would know the outcome soon enough. A tall, lanky weasel entered the saloon and sat down opposite Trask. He had sharply defined features and had a habit of hooding his eyes when he talked, a gesture that unnerved Trask somewhat. His name was Waco. He was not a member of the Shackleton gang, but he did work for Shackleton and Wendell Trask from time to time.

He made Trask's skin crawl.

Waco signaled to the bartender, who came over to the table with a bottle of whiskey and left it there.

"Did you get word on Blackjack?" Waco asked.

"That lady doctor is tending to him right now," Trask said. "I sent Taggart and Curly Bob to go with him. It's in the Lord's hands."

"That is a comforting thought," Waco said, with no trace of irony. He looked around the saloon. "Kind of quiet in here."

"Folks are over to the Music Theater listening to that singer, Missy Vartan," Trask said. "That will give us some breathing space while the doctor tries to dig that bullet out of Blackjack's hide."

Waco looked back at Trask. "If Shackleton dies, you gonna take over the reins of the outfit?"

"It might come to that. Were you thinking of throwing in with us?"

"We'll have to see how the hand plays out."

There was a burst of laughter from the Music Theater down the street.

"Sounds as if folks are having a good time," Trask said.

The Musical Hall Theater was packed with guests. The lights came down and there was applause. Missy Vartan stepped into a spotlight. She was dressed in a scoop neck floor- length chiffon lace dress decorated with beaded sequins. She looked absolutely gorgeous. A backdrop of a New England scene brightened around her. Her pianist, seated at a piano on the stage, began to play. Missy started singing and her voice was beautiful, crystal-clear and carried out into the moonlit night. Homer was sitting at the end of an aisle beside his father, Deke Reneker. Seated in the row behind them were Sheriff Tom Shaw and Alice. Skeeter sat beside her mother. Tom Shaw listened to Missy's ballad with rapturous enjoyment.

At the edge of town, inside Dr. Drake's house, the outlaws stood around the kitchen table. Curly Bob was looking down at Blackjack Shackleton, holding a leather belt. Taggart leaned in with a bottle in one hand.

"Put the belt in his mouth," Rachel instructed Curly Bob, "so he can bite down on it, and hold him still." She turned to Taggart. "Pour the laudanum down his throat first, but don't let him choke on it."

Curly Bob glanced over at Taggart. "Does she know what the hell she's doing?"

"Shut up and do what the doctor tells you," Taggart said.

"She ain't no doctor," Curly Bob insisted.

"I'll remember that the next time you get gut shot," Taggart retorted.

Taggart poured the liquid down Shackleton's throat as Rachel held open his mouth. He sputtered and coughed, moaning in pain. She bought a gleaming scalpel down to the gaping bullet wound.

5

Doc Holiday

IN THE MUSIC HALL THEATER, Missy Vartan sang another song, one in which she encouraged the audience to join. Her violinist and oboist were accompanying her now. The audience was held spellbound. The chair next to Deke Reneker was vacant. Skeeter looked around and saw that Homer was missing. She turned to her mother.

"That no good ruffian Homer is gone," she whispered. "I'll bring him back!"

Alice was alarmed. She whispered: "Skeeter!"

But Skeeter was out of her seat.

Outside in the street, Homer was running past the Last Chance Saloon. Lightning erupted over him. Thunder cracked like a distant explosion. A light rain had begun to fall. Skeeter exited the theater and caught sight of the boy.

"Homer!" she called out. "You come back here!"

He paid no attention to her. Skeeter ran after him out into the sheeting rain.

Inside Dr. Drake's house, Rachel dropped a bloody bullet into a tin cup. "I will stitch up the wound," she said. "More laudanum."

Taggart went to fetch the laudanum. Curly Bob looked down at Shackleton. He was unconscious and as white as a sheet. "He gonna expire on us?"

"He could die right on this table," Rachel said.

Curly Bob took the gun from his holster. "That happens, Doctor, *you* die."

"Get that gun out of my face or you can watch him die," she said.

Paul Taggart returned with a bottle of laudanum, grabbed the gun out of Curly Bob's hand and roughly holstered it.

"Make another move on the doc and I'll gut-shoot you myself. Unless you are fixin' to take over the reins from Blackjack if you see he is slipping away."

"Nothing like that," Curly Bob said. "The doc is doing a fine job."

"No thanks to you," Taggart said. He looked down at Blackjack Shackleton. "Is he gonna make it?"

"Let us see if he makes it through the night," Rachel said.

"I'm obliged to you," Taggart said.

"Can you carry him into the spare bedroom?" Rachel asked.

"Yes, ma'am."

Taggart and Curly Bob lifted Shackleton up and carried him out of the front room.

In Retribution, Doc Holliday's cottage was in shadows. Homer crept up to it. There were no lights on in the house. By that time Skeeter had finally caught up with him. She practically shook him like he was a rat she had found at the side of the road.

"What is the matter with you, Homer?" she demanded. "That Missy Vartan's got a voice like an angel come to visit us. What in the world are you doin' here?"

"I always wanted to see where Doc's house was," Homer said. "I guess Doc ain't home. He's probably at the concert."

Skeeter let him go while she thought about a suitable punishment for him. She shook her head. "No, I'd have noticed him."

"Let's see what's inside," Homer said.

He started forward but Skeeter grabbed his arm. "You can't go sneaking into someone's home!"

"You want to see what's in there badly as I do!"

Homer ducked under Skeeter's arm and raced to the front of the darkened house.

"Homer, no!" Skeeter cried out.

It was too late. Homer was already there. The front door was locked. Skeeter was beside him in an instant. Homer raised one of the front windows just enough for him to scramble through. Skeeter sighed, shook her head helplessly and went after him.

Inside Dr. Drake's house, the outlaws were gathered. In the front room, Shackleton's breathing was shallow, but it was marginally better than the ragged death rattle that the outlaws had heard before. His wound was now heavily bandaged. Curly Bob was looking at Rachel with new respect. She wiped her hands on a linen cloth.

"What happens now, Doc?" Taggart asked her.

"We wait," Rachel replied. "His fever is high and it's gotta break. I do not want you two breathing over him. Find somewhere to go."

"We'll be at the Crystal Palace Saloon," Taggart told her. "Are you expecting anyone to come and call tonight?"

"Not unless there's an emergency in town," Rachel said.

"Everyone's at a concert at the Music Hall Theater," Curly Bob said.

"Have Jake come and get us when Mr. Shackleton wakes up," Taggart said. Then he added: "Or he dies."

Rachel just nodded. Taggart and Curly Bob left. Outside the house, Taggart and Curly Bob mounted their horses. Taggart looked at Jake Turnbull.

"I'll leave you here with Dr. Drake. Do not go into the house. Let Blackjack sweat it out. If you need to find us, we will be at the Crystal Palace Saloon. And do not bother the doc none. If I hear anything has happened to her, I'll shoot first and ask questions later."

"What if someone comes visitin'?" Turnbull asked.

"Deal with it," Taggart said, shortly.

He and Curly Bob rode away from Dr. Drake's house.

Inside, Rachel moved into the small bedroom and looked down at Shackleton. His breathing was still labored and he was sleeping. Rachel leaned down to him. Her voice was barely above a whisper.

"My husband Samuel was a decent man. Caring and compassionate. Which of your outlaws killed him? Taggart or Curly Bob? It does not matter. I will find out. And Samuel will have some kind of justice. If I have to pull the trigger myself."

She straightened and noted that her hands were shaking.

Blackjack Shackleton did not stir in his troubled sleep.

Inside Doc Holliday's cottage, Homer and Skeeter prowled through the myriad shadows. Skeeter paused to admire a half-finished painting mounted on an easel of the Arizona desert while Homer surreptitiously went through the drawers of the bureau in the bedroom. Skeeter did not see what Homer was doing at first.

"Look at this painting!" Skeeter exclaimed, raising her voice."It's beautiful!" She looked down at the canvas and noted a signature that said: *D. Holliday.* "There is Doc's signature at the bottom! I never knew Doc was a painter. The colors are exquisite! Look at these brushstrokes. Very delicate! You listening to me, you ruffian rat?"

"Sure, I am," he said from the bedroom, going through the bottom drawers of the bureau.

"You are not getting into trouble in there, are you?"

"Just looking around," he said, carelessly.

"I'll bet Doc has more of these paintings!" Skeeter said. "Look over here!"

Skeeter found some more paintings stacked on two easels. Most of them were half-finished. She gingerly went through another sunset and a San Francisco street setting where the cable cars were gorgeous. She noted another painting where two Confederate soldiers were looking through binoculars at a rushing river. Beside it was a painting of Union soldiers standing outside the Palace Bar with a couple saying goodbye in the foreground and a stagecoach thundering through a canyon gorge. Skeeter found more canvases stacked in an oil cloth behind another easel. Some of them were half-completed landscapes but a couple of them were portraits of townspeople in Retribution. She found a painting of a young girl, about ten years old, with long dark hair curled in little ringlets. Skeeter thought it looked a little like her, but her face was not the same. She found an almost completed small canvas titled: *RETRIBUTION SUNSET* which depicted vivid blood-red fingers of dying light reaching across Saratoga Street.

"Never seen the town in these colors," Skeeter remarked. "No people on the boardwalks. No horses at the hitchin' posts. It is like the town is dying along with the sun and when darkness comes it will be a ghost town. So maybe you are right, Homer." She sighed. "Maybe Doc is not a real gunfighter at all. Maybe them's all stories."

In the bedroom, Homer was suddenly triumphant. "Oh, yeah? Then what is a painter doing with this?"

He ran back in from the bedroom. Skeeter scrambled over to him. Homer paused, looking at the oil painting of the young girl which Skeeter pulled out from the others. "Is that you?"

"'Course not, Homer! Why would I be in a painting in Doc Holliday's house? Just a tolerable likeness. What have you got there?

Homer had taken out a thick gun belt from a bottom bureau drawer, wrapped in cashmere. He put it almost reverently on a table. Skeeter unwrapped the gun belt, revealing a pearl-handled Colt .45 revolver in the holster. She gave a low whistle. "I knew it! Check out the pearl handle. Doc *is* a gunfighter, just like folks say!"

Homer was agog with excitement. "How many men do ya think Doc has killed with this gun?"

Doc's voice echoed behind them. "It might be twelve if I was counting, which I'm not."

Both of the kids froze and swung around. Doc strode toward them from the back patio. He picked up the gun belt, wrapped the cashmere cloth around it and returned it to the bottom drawer in the bedroom. Homer cowered back, ready to bolt. Skeeter grabbed his arm, holding her ground. Doc returned to his front room and looked at them balefully, but there was a glimmer of humor in his eyes.

"Why do you have a second gun?" Skeeter asked.

"The pearl-handled gun is more of a keepsake. It was given to me in Dodge City by the City Council. I do not have call to use it."

"But you still have your Colt .45 revolver handy?" Homer said.

"I do. If that is any of your business, which it ain't. What are you two doing in here?"

"I'm sorry, Doc," Skeeter said. "It wasn't Homer, he... I mean, it was *me*. I wanted to look around. It was wrong to come into your home uninvited. We deserve whatever punishment you choose to serve up to us."

"I'd better give that some careful thought," Doc replied, judiciously.

"You gotta finish that painting of Retribution at sunset!" Skeeter blurted out. "It is gorgeous. Gave me chills."

"I see you have been looking at more of my paintings."

"I couldn't help myself! That painting of the Confederate soldiers standing at the river looking through binoculars, you could hear the wind rushing across through the reeds! And where those two sweethearts are saying goodbye outside the Palace Bar sure took my fancy."

Homer picked out the painting of a stagecoach. "I like this one! Where is that stagecoach headed?"

"Cathedral Rock in the Arizona territory."

"It is beautiful," Skeeter said. "It takes your breath away."

"I am glad you liked them," Doc said, his irritation having somewhat subsided.

He took the painting from Homer's hands and carefully placed it back among the other paintings. Skeeter shook her head. "The places you have been to, Doc..."

"Mainly in my imagination."

He picked up his .45 revolver in its holster that was lying on a table on the patio. Homer stood his ground, as if challenging Doc. "If you are a real gunfighter, can you teach me how to shoot?"

Skeeter slapped Homer on the back of the head, not quite hard enough to knock him through the floor. "Hush now, Homer!"

"It is unlikely that you would ever need to pull a gun on someone," Doc said.

"My father is the sheriff," Skeeter said, "but I don't reckon he's ever pulled leather in his life. Just give us a demonstration, Doc," she pleaded. "So if Tom Shaw does ever find himself reaching for his gun, maybe you can make sure he don't get shot before he can pull his gun out of its holster. I would consider it a kindness."

Doc looked at them both and considered their proposal.

Inside the Musical Hall Theater, Missy Vartan finished her performance to tumultuous applause. Several of the cowboys fired their guns into a ceiling already pock-marked with bullet holes. Missy bowed, acknowledging her pianist, oboist and violinist, who also took their bows. Deke Reneker was standing, his eyes shining. Alice Shaw politely applauded, looking for Skeeter. Tom Shaw was standing, clapping appreciatively along with Mayor Ballantyne, Swede and his wife.

Inside the Crystal Palace Saloon, the non-concert crowd and cowboys were at the tables, saloon girls moving among them. Paul Taggart and Curly Bob were at a table. Jim Plank set a bottle of whiskey and glasses in front of them. It was clear he recognized the outlaws, even though he tried to act casual.

"Did not see you at first," he said. "First drinks are on the house, gents. Compliments of Deke Reneker." He poured them two shots. "If you are here for the big concert, I reckon it's about over."

"Too bad we missed it," Taggart said, sarcastically.

"Maybe you are just passin' through Retribution?"

"Maybe we like it here," Curly Bob said. "Looks like a nice, friendly town."

Taggart threw some money on the table. Jim Plank left them alone. He went back to the bar where he whispered something to a young bartender named Billy. Billy nodded and moved behind the bar. Plank took off his bar apron and exited. Taggart looked at his Eglin pocket watch which featured a Greek Goddess engraved in silver.

"Should be time for Trask to ride out to the Drake place," he said.

Kyle Bascomb rode into Retribution. The storm that had threatened the town had blown itself out. Kyle headed to Doc Holliday's cottage. The walls were high enough that no one could see in. There was an outdoor patio. The last time Kyle had been there to see Doc Holliday, he had noted an easel had been set up in the patio.

Inside the house, Doc led the way into the patio which had a red flagstone floor filled with cactus plants. The painting Doc was currently working on was of a cowboy on a beach, his horse at the water's edge at sunrise. He put a couple of tin cans onto a low brick wall. Homer waited, barely able to contain his excitement. Skeeter was examining the painting on Doc's easel.

"Ain't never been to a beach," she said. "You know this particular cowboy?"

"Probably one of Doc's victims," Homer said.

Skeeter smacked him on the head without looking at him. She was watching Doc closely. "Can't be easy to kill a man."

"Shadows move," Doc said, "and in them are the splinters of men's greed and vengeance and callousness. When they move, you have to be ready."

"For what?" Skeeter asked.

"A leap of faith," Doc said.

He picked up a nickel-plated gun from a table, turned around and blew the two cans off the wall without even appearing to aim at them.

Skeeter applauded vigorously. "Wow, shit!" Doc looked at her. "Language. Sorry."

"Shooting tin cans and shooting at a fellow human being are very different," Doc said. "Remember that distinction, Homer."

Homer gulped and nodded. Skeeter looked at Doc with hero worship in her eyes. "I bet you never miss!" she said, breathlessly.

"Depends what I am aimin' at. I reckon it is time for you two to go home."

"Let us stay a little longer," Skeeter pleaded. "We are good company, ain't we?"

Doc finally suppressed a smile. "Tolerable," he said.

The town hall across the street from the Musical Hall Theater had been decorated for a party. Long buffet tables were filled with food and large glass punch bowls. The atmosphere was festive. A banner had been hoisted over a raised stage that said: *WELCOME MISSY VARTAN* --

SONGBIRD OF EUROPE AND THE AMERICAS. Mayor Ballantyne was greeting the townspeople at the door. Missy Vartan and her entourage were at the center of attention, shaking hands, accepting glasses of punch and wine, talking animatedly.

On the outskirts of town, Dr. Drake's house was lit up. Paul Trask rode up and dismounted. He had a brief word with Jake Turnbull, who rode away. Trask entered the house. Rachel emerged from the living room. She did not recognize Trask, but she knew instinctively that he was part of Blackjack Shackleton's gang.

"I need to see your patient," Trask said.

"He can't be disturbed right now," Rachel said. "He's sleeping."

"Wake him up."

Before Rachel could stop him, Trask moved to the closed door to the bedroom and threw it open. Shackleton was, indeed, sleeping fitfully. Rachel came up behind Trask. He looked down at Blackjack.

"What if I was to take him out of here and put him on horseback?"

"You might kill him," Rachel said. "He is my patient and he can't be moved."

"Looks like you did a good job of patchin' him up," Trask said.

"I am a doctor. I try to heal the sick. If his condition worsens I will let you know. Now get out of my house."

Trask moved through the front room. Rachel followed him. Trask turned suddenly and ran his hand from her waist up over her right breast. Rachel looked reflexively at a drawer in a desk, not quite within her reach. Trask gripped her throat.

"You'd be dead before you could touch the gun in that drawer," he said, softly.

"Is that what happened to my husband?" Rachel asked him.

That gave Trask pause. Finally he eased off her. "Don't know anything about your late husband. Tend to your patient. I will be right outside."

Trask let her go and let himself out through the front door. Rachel took a deep breath and slowly let it out again.

In Retribution, on Doc's patio, Skeeter pulled a cloth off the unfinished painting she had found of a young girl about 10 years old on Doc's easel.

"You should sell your paintings," Homer suggested. "My dad would put them up at the Crystal Palace."

"They're not for sale," Doc said.

"Must be lonely, painting memories no one else will see," Skeeter said. "Your family ever visit you? The little girl in your painting looks just like you, except her eyes are real sad."

"Her name was Jenny," Doc finally said. "She died of smallpox when she was three. Her ma, too. I tried to imagine what she would look like today, a couple of years younger than you, Skeeter."

"How come you ain't finished it?" Homer wanted to know.

"He will finish it," Skeeter said. "I know you will, Doc."

Doc suddenly picked up his gun from the patio without turning around, then set it back down.

"Evening, Marshal."

Kyle Bascomb walked onto the patio of Doc's house. A smile creased his face. "Doc, I didn't think you heard me."

"A mistake more than one lawman has made," Doc commented, dryly.

Kyle looked over at Skeeter and Homer. "Where did you get the family?"

Doc made the introductions. "Homer belongs to Deke Reneker. He owns the Crystal Palace Saloon in Retribution among other things. This young lady answers to the name of Abigail, but folks call her Skeeter. She is the daughter of Sheriff Tom Shaw."

"Pleased to make your acquaintance, Marshal," Skeeter said.

Homer was excited. "What brings you here to Retribution?"

"The Marshal don't have to explain himself to you, Homer!" Skeeter said, mildly.

"Bet you got a warrant here for Doc!"

Homer ducked the smack he knew he was going to get from Skeeter. "Homer, mind your manners!" she said, as if she was scandalized. She turned to Kyle. "He don't mean nothing by it, Marshal. Sometimes his mouth doesn't seem to be connected to his brain."

"There might be an outstanding warrant in one in my saddlebags," Kyle allowed. Now Skeeter was excited in spite of herself. "You here to call Doc out, Marshal?"

Kyle shook his head. "I am in Retribution just to visit an old friend," he said.

"But if you did call Doc out," Homer said, "which of you would be faster pulling leather?"

"We've never had to find out," Kyle said, as if amused.

Skeeter grabbed Homer's hand, yanking him toward the ajar gate in the wooden fence. "Goodnight, Doc," she said. "Goodnight, Marshal. They are having a big party for that Songbird of Europe and the Americas over at the town hall. Everyone is invited. We don't get there, we'll get paddled."

Skeeter scooted Homer through the open gate out into the night.

"Looks like those kids are pretty taken with you," Kyle said.

"I don't encourage it," Doc said. "I heard your posse ran down Blackjack Shackleton but couldn't hold onto him."

"He left with a bullet in his gut. I do not reckon he'll be holding up any banks this side of Christmas."

"So you are not here in Retribution to settle that score with him?"

"I am not."

Doc moved back over to the painting of the sunset and added some brushstrokes to it. "Watch your back, Marshal. Blackjack Shackleton is a treacherous ruffian."

"I will keep that in mind."

"It has been some time since we have seen each other," Doc remarked.

"Has."

"You here for me?"

"Nope."

"So this a social call?"

"You can call it that. I ain't got too many friends I can count on anymore. Just wanted to renew the friendship."

"Appreciate that sentiment," Doc said. "I hear you were riding on a posse headed by Jefferson Forrester that turned into a bloodbath."

"It did."

"Did you catch up with Forrester?"

"I did."

"Where was that?"

"In a town called Fargo Springs. He sent a shooter to my hotel room. I had some help from Wyatt Earp."

"Wyatt Earp is a good man to have on your side," Doc said. "Did you confront Jefferson Forrester?"

"I did."

"What happened?"

"I shot him dead."

Doc nodded. "Glad to hear that. He was a back shooter and a coward. How long will you be in staying in Retribution?"

"Long as it takes to sweet talk a young woman into leaving with me," Kyle said.

Doc was ironic. "Guess that might take a while."

"Maybe we'll pass each other in the street of Retribution like strangers."

"Might," Doc allowed.

Doc stared to cough rackingly. He pulled out a blood-stained handkerchief and put it to his lips. The coughing fit passed. Doc leaned against the easel.

Kyle said: "I hear the sulfur vapors at Glenwood Springs can be meritorious for consumption."

"I'll surely keep that in mind," Doc said.

"Maybe I will see you over at the Crystal Palace Saloon one night."

Doc returned to his painting. "Might. But I am not in the habit of entertaining lawmen. Goodnight, Marshal."

Kyle tipped his hat and exited through the gate, shutting it behind him.

6

Sheriff Tom Shaw

INSIDE THE TOWN HALL the opening night party for Missy Vartan and her musicians was in full swing. Missy was suffering patiently in the company of Mayor Ballantyne and a couple of City Council members.

"It is not every night a luminary of your distinction has graced us with your presence," the mayor gushed. "Could be I bold enough to ask you if would consider a return engagement before you left Retribution?"

"That would be charming, Major Ballantyne, but I have commitments in St. Louis and Philadelphia to fulfill."

"The town council would make it worth your while to stay just one day longer," the mayor cajoled. "Isn't that right, Mr. Reneker?"

Missy looked imploringly at Deke for help. He watched the exchange, amused.

"We would be happy to extend your stay in Retribution for as long as you want," Deke told her, graciously.

Missy glared at him, trapped. The mayor and the other council members crowded around her. Jim Plank moved up to Deke, took him to one side and whispered in his ear. Deke looked at him. "How many of the out-laws?"

"Just the two of 'em," Plank said. "Paul Taggart and Curly Bob. They are in the Crystal Palace Saloon right now. But I don't reckon they don't go nowhere without Blackjack Shackleton."

"And where is he?"

"Gut-shot on the road," Plank said. "Rachel is treating him right now at her house outside of town. I heard the outlaws talking. I figured you would want to know about it."

"Your consideration is noted," Deke said. "Leave this with me. Let me know if Shackleton's men get anywhere near the town hall."

"Will you send Tom Shaw against them?"

Deke looked at Plank as if he were an idiot. "Not if I want to see our erstwhile sheriff get himself killed. This is the right setting for him. He can preen and pontificate in an affair like this with little chance of getting caught up in a gunfight." He glanced over at Missy Vartan. "Under no circumstances should anything happen to our guest of honor. You might stop by the sheriff's office and let Otis Larchmont know what is going on."

"Will do, boss," Plank said.

Deke Reneker dismissed him with a careless wave of his hand.

A moment later Missy Vartan took his place, a glass of champagne in her hand. She was happy she had escaped the saccharine platitudes of the mayor and his cronies. She looked at Jim Plank as he moved away from Deke. Her expression was ironic. "I see you still have your pet weasel working for you?"

"Jim Plank has been a good friend. Seen me through some rough patches. You never got to know him. You would have taken a shine to him if you had."

She looked back at Deke. "Something is going on that none of the guests know about. I can feel it."

"It is nothing for you to worry about," Deke said. His gaze swept over the room. "Just look at the turnout for your opening night! The men adore you and the women envy you."

"You haven't answered my question," Missy said.

"Just enjoy your night, Missy. You have earned it."

Deke moved away from her. Missy Vartan looked after him. She took another swallow of champagne, her eyes troubled.

Inside Dr. Drake's house, Rachel was wiping sweat from Shackleton's forehead with a damp cloth. His eyes were open. His breathing was better. He tried to rise, but Rachel gently forced him back down.

"You can't move yet," Rachel said. "The bullet's out, but you've lost a lot of blood."

Shackleton's voice was ragged. "Folks here find out you saved me they might just come calling with torches and burn you out."

"Deke Reneker won't let that happen."

"So, he is still the one to be reckoned with in Retribution," Shackleton said. "He still running the Crystal Palace Saloon?"

"He is."

Shackleton looked at Rachel's face. "Your husband got killed in his saloon, didn't he?"

Rachel's voice now had an edge to it. "How do you know that?"

"Seem to recall one of my boys did the shooting. Over a poker hand. Your husband was tryin' to win enough money to take both of you back east."

"Samuel was desperate," Rachel said, softly, her voice barely above a whisper.

"You want your revenge," Shackleton told her. "I can appreciate that. You can rip this bandage off me right now and I'll bleed to death."

"Any reason why I shouldn't?" she asked.

"None that I can see."

"Why'd you tell me?"

"Wanted to get it off my chest."

For a moment Rachel did not move. Then she continued to wipe down Shackleton's face and arms. "Your fever needs to break."

Wendell Trask stepped out of the shadows of the room, looking down at Shackleton. "Good to see you awake," he said. "How are you feeling?"

"Tolerable."

"I will tell the others."

"Take your time, I ain't goin' anywhere," Shackleton said. "I will be ready to ride in the morning."

"That isn't going to happen," Rachel said. "You need at least forty-hours of sleep."

"I am leaving here *in the morning*," Shackleton repeated. Then he looked up at Rachel. "Unless you are aimin' to ride into Retribution and bring back the law here with you."

Rachel shook her head. "I wouldn't do that."

"Wouldn't do you much good," Trask said. He looked back at Shackleton. "The town sheriff is a joke. Name is Tom Shaw. From what I can see he struts around looking important. He wouldn't be any threat."

Shackleton settled back down. Rachel pulled the covers on the bed around him. "You need to rest now," she said.

Trask left the room. There was a silence while Rachel wrestled with her emotions. Finally she said: "Was Trask the gunman who killed my husband?"

Shackleton's diseased eyes looked up at her. They told Rachel everything she wanted to know.

In the main street of Retribution three of Shackleton's outlaws dismounted, tethered their horses, and entered the Crystal Palace Saloon. Down the street, at the town hall, Skeeter and Homer arrived at the party. Homer made a beeline for one of the buffet tables and started to pile food onto a plate. Skeeter was intercepted by her mother. Alice's tone was half-scolding and half-frightened.

"Where have you been, young lady?"

"Looking after Homer," Skeeter said, which was half true.

"I have been looking for you everywhere!" Alice said. "Your father has been wanting me to introduce you to the cream of society for once and you are nowhere to be seen! What has happened to your manners?"

"I am sorry, Ma. We were over to Doc's place and…"

"I will not have you consorting with gunfighters!" Alice said, her voice raising a little too loud.

"Doc is my friend," Skeeter said, hotly. "He is gentlemanly and considerate and would never do anything to hurt me! He is the best friend I got next to Homer, and maybe then some. Don't you want me to have friends, Ma?"

"Of course I do! But your own age! Not some alcoholic killer who has taken a shine to you! You are not to see him again!"

Alice Shaw was in such a state that Skeeter suddenly took pity on her. She knew that her mother was reacting to the pressures that living in Retribution had inflicted on her. She was even more emotional and distraught than Skeeter had realized. Skeeter took her hand into hers.

"I am sorry, Ma. I will be more careful who I associate with. I know you are only looking out for me." She looked past her mother. "There's your friend Sonia from the sewing club. Why don't you go and talk to her and I will make sure that no-good Homer leaves some food for the rest of the guests."

Skeeter ran on to the buffet table. Alice started to follow, but Tom Shaw waved at her to join him where he was standing with Missy Vartan and Deke Reneker. Reluctantly Alice did so, putting on a brave face for the rest of the guests.

Skeeter found Homer piling his plate high with food. He glanced past her. "Your ma was talking to you in a sing-song voice and that always means trouble."

"She is going to be fine," Skeeter said, determinedly. "And don't go feeding your face like this was your last meal on earth! Lordy, I don't know which of you is worse, you or my mother!"

Homer just shrugged and grinned.

Down the street in the Crystal Palace Saloon, Otis Larchmont, Tom Shaw's deputy, sat at a table in the back, drinking beer. Shackleton's three gunmen joined Taggart at his table and were drinking whiskey. Curly Bob sat another table having a violent argument with a cowboy. The cowboy got up and threw a punch at Curly Bob. Curly Bob drew his gun in one swift motion and fired, killing the man. The cowboy's friend, sitting at the same table, reached for his gun. Paul Taggart fired without getting up from his table. The friend fell to the floor, dead. The tables on either side cleared, but then everyone went back to their drinks and conversation. Otis Larchmont was on his feet, but instead of attempting to arrest the outlaws, he hurried out the swing doors. Billy, who was tending bar, had one of the saloon girls help him haul the two bodies behind the bar away from sight.

At Rachel's house, pale moonlight streamed through the windows. She moved through the house with a gun now in her hand. A figure stepped out of the shadows and grabbed her.

It was Kyle Bascomb.

He took the weapon from Rachel's hand and set it on the kitchen table.

"Must be a dangerous patient if you have to guard him with a gun."

"Kyle!" she said, softly.

She moved into his arms and kissed him passionately. When they broke, she held him at arm's length, as if she had just lost him forever.

"I didn't think you'd come back," she said.

"Told you I would," Kyle said.

But Rachel was edgy. "Let us talk out on the porch."

"Right here is fine," Kyle said. "I am handing in my badge to the Governor of the Territories. I thought I might try some prospecting in Oregon. Come with me, Rachel."

She pulled away from him. "I've thought about this moment. That you came back and took me in your arms and my wondering if there could be a future for us. But here, Kyle. Right here in Retribution."

"This ain't a town I could settle down into."

"If Doc Holliday can settle here, so can you! Did you know he was living in Retribution?"

"I did," Kyle said. "Doc has demons he has to fight alone. Mine are chasing me." Something in Rachel's tension had alerted him. "What's wrong?"

"I'm just surprised to see you, that's all."

On an impulse Kyle pushed past her toward the bedroom.

"Kyle! Don't go in there!"

Rachel followed him, but she was too late. Kyle pushed open the door and saw Blackjack John Shackleton lying on the bed with the covers pulled around him. He was sleeping. Kyle stopped dead, staring down at the outlaw. Rachel entered the bedroom behind him.

"You know who this is?" Kyle asked, softly.

"Yes," she said. "And I have every reason in the world to want him dead. He or one of his men killed Samuel. But right now he is under my care. Once he sets foot out the front door, you can hang him in front of the livery stable for all I care. Or do you have to turn him over to Marshal Forrester?"

"Marshal Jackson Forrester is dead," Kyle said. "He drew down on me when I was in a town called Fargo Springs."

"He was gunning for you?"

"He was."

Rachel nodded. "What are you going to do about Shackleton?"

"I will hand him to the local sheriff here in Retribution."

"You'll be sorry if you do," Rachel said.

Kyle looked at her. "Why is that?"

"Because the sheriff here is named Tom Shaw and he could not go against these outlaws. Shackleton has brought most of his gang with him."

"Good to know." Kyle looked once more on the sleeping figure of Blackjack Shackleton, then he gently closed the door of the bedroom. He took Rachel's hand. "We need to talk."

In Retribution at the town hall where Missy Vartan's Opening party was being held, Deputy Otis Larchmont pushed his way through the festive crowd to where Mayor Ballantyne was holding court. Deke Reneker stood beside him, keeping the champagne flowing. Tom Shaw was in earnest conversation with some members of Mayor Ballantyne's staff, expounding on the virtues of keeping law and order paramount in their minds. Alice Shaw had found her friend Sonia who was listening about the importance of keeping the schoolhouse open and full. Mayor Ballantyne was saying: "It is with a great deal of pride that I can announce that Miss Vartan has graciously agreed to extend her engagement in our exquisite Music Hall Theater for a second night and…"

Otis gripped Tom Shaw's arm, cutting off the conversation. "Sheriff, five of John Shackleton's men are in the Crystal Place. Two of them gunned down Pete McCoy and that prospector pal of his. I saw the whole thing."

"But you did nothing to stop it," Deneker said, contemptuously. "Have any more of my customers been cut down by stray outlaw bullets?"

"Taggart and Curly Bob went back to drinking like nothing had happened," Otis said.

Various conversations within the room were petering out. Skeeter and Homer pushed through to the front. All eyes were on Sheriff Tom Shaw. He squared his shoulders, taking one last swallow of champagne, then raised his voice.

"I will deputize anyone who is willing to walk over to the Crystal Palace Saloon with me and rid our town of this vermin. Five silver dollars a man. All right, Mr. Mayor?"

Mayor Ballantyne was trying to impress Missy Vartan. "Ten!" he said.

Sheriff Shaw looked around the room. No one moved. He nodded. "Looks like it's up to us, Otis."

Alice gripped her husband's hand. "Thomas, no! You cannot go up against these killers!"

"I am the sheriff, Alice," he said, stiffly. He produced a wan smile for the guests. "I have a duty to perform."

Sheriff Shaw and Otis moved through the silent crowd, which parted for them, and both men walked out the door into the street. Tears flooded Alice Shaw's eyes. Beside her there was sudden terror in Skeeter's eyes.

Outside Dr. Drake's house, Kyle Bascomb looked to-ward the lights of Retribution. Rachel entered behind him.

"There was a gunman who was on guard here out-side the house," she said.

Kyle nodded. "Wendell Trask. Ran into him in Wich-ita. A backshooter."

"He might be gathering the other members of Shack-leton's gang together. They could be back here in half an hour."

"More like a couple of hours," Kyle said. "Time for them to let off some steam, play some poker, get drunk. Their boss ain't going anywhere."

"We need to talk, Kyle," Rachel said. "There is a lot we have to say to each other."

"I know."

"But now I can't find the right words."

"Maybe there aren't any words that measure up to the feelings we're experiencing," he said. "We were apart for a long time. That was mostly my fault." He looked at her. "Nothin's going to bring Samuel back. You know that. You gotta move on with your life, Rachel."

"I did," Rachel said. "I haven't been waiting for you. I have patients who need me. I cannot abandon them."

"Because they've accepted you," Kyle said. "Because you are a woman doctor. Somewhere else, folks might not be so liberal and accommodating."

She took his hand. Her voice was emotional. "I know your heart. You care about people. You are always going to be a peace officer. You turn in your Marshal's badge and they will just deputize you in some other lawless prairie town. I will be in a nice little house with a fence and a vegetable garden and maybe even a kid like Skeeter waiting for someone to tell me that you are lying sprawled in the street after a gunfight."

Kyle nodded. He had no easy answer for her. "Could be that way," he allowed. He looked through the ajar front door with a crooked smile. "'Least I'll have a wife who could dig a bullet out of my hide."

"There is that notion," Rachel said, smiling now through her tears. "But how long would it be for men like Blackjack Shackleton to call you out to address some wrong in their lives? You are a marshal, whether you hand in your badge or not. Are you still friendly with Wyatt Earp?"

"I would count him as a friend."

"He quit being a marshal in Dodge City sometime ago. I talked to Hoss Cavanaugh in Retribution who said that Wyatt Earp was going to be the new marshal in Tombstone."

"He said nothing to me about it when our paths crossed recently."

"Because he *needs* to be a marshal," Rachel said, "He will accept that Marshal's badge when the time is right for him. Just like the way you will. There is nothing I can do to stop it. It is part of your soul."

"Maybe we don't have to settle this discussion to-night," Kyle said. "Right now you have got the worst killer in the territory sweating out a fever in your spare bed-room. That's a situation we both have to deal with."

Rachel extricated her arm from Kyle's. She looked through the storm haze toward Retribution. "If you are going to take Blackjack Shackleton out of here, you'd bet-ter do it soon."

7

Shootout

OUT ON THE BACK PATIO of Doc Holliday's cottage, bright moonlight filtered through the storm clouds. Doc had the oil canvas of the '*Retribution Sunset*' on the easel. He dabbed at the oranges and reds creeping across the empty main street of the painting. Doc's revolver was still laid out on a table. Skeeter burst through the unlocked gate and ran up to Doc. Words came tumbling out of her.

"Doc, they're going to kill him! They are going to kill my father!"

"Slow down, Skeeter," Doc said. "Who's going to kill your father?"

Skeeter caught her breath. "Some outlaws at the Crystal Palace. They already gunned down Pete McCoy, he was the barber, and that old prospector, Silas Bill I think his name was, and my father and his deputy are on their way to the saloon and they do not stand a chance."

Doc turned his attention back to his painting of the sunset. "I seem to recall that your daddy once drew down on three members of the Black Hand gang in a saloon in Deadwood and killed all three of'em."

Skeeter's tone was desperate now. "It did not happen that way! My father shot one the outlaws by accident, the second had his gun jam and the third outlaw tripped and fell into a shotgun blast that came from behind."

"How do you know all that?" Doc asked her, curious.

"Because I was hiding under the stairs in the #10 Saloon in Deadwood when that shootout happened," Skeeter said. "I must have been four years old. Stories get told and retold until they are like cotton candy spun out at the fair. Nothing to them."

Doc applied more paint on his brush. "Tom Shaw is the sheriff of Retribution. It is his fight."

Skeeter was pleading with him. "You could back him up!"

Doc ignored her. She grabbed his arm, so he could no longer paint. "You've got to help him!"

Doc said: "I've got to paint and restrain my more impetuous impulses. Your father has a duty to perform as the sheriff of this town. Let him do it."

Skeeter cried out. "No! No! You cannot let that happen. Don't let him die!"

Doc's voice was gentler. "Nothing I can do about it. You best stay out of the Crystal Palace Saloon, Skeeter."

Skeeter threw herself onto him, beating at his chest with her fists. Tears streamed down her face. "You're a coward! You'd let a good man get killed because he's livin' up to a legend he don't deserve. You should know all about that! I hate you! I hope you die from that cough!"

Doc let her pound on him without trying to catch her wildly flailing arms. Then she stumbled away and ran out the ajar patio gate. Doc set down his paintbrush. He took in a long breath and let it out. He looked at the town of *Retribution* in the dying sunset on the canvas. Then he picked up his .45 Colt revolver from the table, slid it into the small of his back, buttoned his frock coat over it and moved to the patio door.

In Dr. Drake's house, the small bedroom was in shadows. Blackjack Shackleton pulled himself out of bed. He was still in pain, but he felt stronger. He put on his torn shirt and moved to the doorway of the room. He noted Kyle sitting on the porch through the ajar front door talking to Rachel, his words indistinct. For a moment Shackleton was caught up in the sense-memory of the wedding slaughter. He saw one of the posse on horseback in the midst of the other lawmen, firing his Colt revolver. He had a vivid recollection of Kyle's face.

Kyle stood up.

Shackleton leapt at the gun that Rachel left on the table, picked it up and started firing. Out on the porch, bullets exploded around Kyle and Rachel. Kyle dragged Rachel down to the porch floor, drawing his gun.

Shackleton stumbled out the back door of the house and practically fell down a sharp incline. He was immediately swallowed up in the darkness. Kyle ran into the doorway. He caught a glimpse of Shackleton's erratic figure running into the night. Kyle fired twice, but he could not tell if he had hit his target or not. He ran out of the house onto the porch where Rachel was still crouched down.

"Stay here till I get back!" Kyle ordered.

He mounted his horse, wheeled it around and galloped off.

Blackjack Shackleton was halfway down the road. He staggered, gasping for breath. A rider approached him fast. Shackleton crawled under some mesquite bushes at the side of the moonlit road. Kyle galloped by. Shackleton crawled out and took off down the road toward Retribution.

Across the street from the Crystal Palace Saloon, Wendell Trask moved into the freight office, which was closed and locked. Quickly he went through the papers on Hoss Cavanaugh's desk. In a bottom drawer he found the blueprints of the *Iron Maiden Stagecoach* and the route it would take. Trask started to make a map of the route.

In one of the rooms on the second floor of the Crystal Palace Saloon, one of the saloon girls was naked, pulling off Paul Taggart's shirt. The door burst open. Curly Bob was in the doorway. Taggart shook his head.

"Your ma never taught you to knock?"

"We're getting quite an audience downstairs," Curly Bob told him. "Word is that the sheriff is on his way."

Taggart was contemptuous. "Sheriff Tom Shaw? That should make me *real* nervous." He turned back to the naked saloon girl. "What's your name, sweetheart?"

"Carol," she said.

"I'll be back in five minutes, darlin'." He turned back to Curly Bob. "I reckon that's about as long as this will take to deal with the sheriff."

Tom Shaw and Otis Larchmont reached the Crystal Palace Saloon. Shaw was carrying a shotgun, Otis a Winchester. They split up, Otis moving toward the back. Shaw stood motionless, the enormity of what he was about to do sinking into him.

Deke Reneker and Jim Plank moved to the side of the saloon. "I wouldn't want the sheriff deprived of his one moment of glory," Deke murmured, "because of his deputy."

Plank said: "I'll take care of it."

He moved after Otis Larchmont. Deke entered the Crystal Place Saloon by a side door. He moved behind the bar. Skeeter and Homer snuck in through the same ajar side door and ducked down under an unoccupied table. The two dead men had been dragged to one side of the staircase. Curly Bob was back at his table. The other three gunmen moved to either side of it.

Doc entered through the side door of the Crystal Palace Saloon and stepped casually to one side. Skeeter's tear-stained face lit up when she saw him. She practically crushed Homer's hand in hers. In a harsh whisper she said: "I knew he'd come!"

Across the street, Kyle dismounted and tied up his horse. He immediately saw Sheriff Tom Shaw standing on the boardwalk outside the Crystal Palace Saloon. He had made his decision and walked inside.

The ambiance in the saloon was lively and boisterous. Up on the second-floor corridor, Otis Larchmont crept forward, rifle in hand to backup the Sheriff. Jim Plank came up behind him, swinging the heavy hilt of a knife against the side of his head. Otis crumpled to the ground, unconscious. Plank quickly picked up his fallen rifle. He moved into Deke's apartment and shut the door behind him,

In the saloon, Tom Shaw took stock of who he was up against. He moved to Curly Bob's table. All of the conversation around him had petered out. Skeeter and Homer hunkered down under their table. Skeeter was watching her father with bated breath, afraid to move. She was memorized by what was unfolding in front of her eyes.

Paul Taggart moved down the second-floor corridor to the stairs leading down to the saloon. He waited there in the shadows.

You could hear a pin drop.

Curly Bob got to his feet, his manner easy and relaxed.

"Fellah drew down on me, Sheriff. Ask anyone in here."

"Two men are dead," Tom Shaw said.

"Yes, sir," Curly Bob said, "and another fellah pulled a gun and my friend shot him before he could put a bullet in me. All self-defense. My friend ain't here right now, but I will make sure he drops by your office and tells you the whole story."

Kyle entered the saloon and mingled with the other spectators. He noted Doc Holliday standing near the stairs. A look passed between them.

Tom Shaw's eyes flickered to the sweeping staircase that led up to the second floor of the saloon. He had expected to see Otis Larchmont standing up there on the balcony with his rifle pointed down into the saloon.

He was not there.

Paul Taggart had stepped back so he was not visible from the saloon floor.

Shaw looked back at Curly Bob. "There is a no-firearms law in Retribution after sundown," he said.

"I must not have seen that sign, sir," Curly Bob said, affably. "Awful sorry about that. We will just finish our drinks and leave."

"Not tonight you won't," Shaw said. "Unbuckle your gun belts. Nice and slow."

Now Curly Bob's good humor had deserted him. His manner became brusque. "There's four of us, Sheriff."

Tom Shaw mustered all the bravado he could. He even managed a smile. "Won't matter to you, Curly Bob.

This shotgun is pointed right at your heart. Now drop those gun belts on the table."

The moment lingered and then---

Curly Bob drew his gun before Tom Shaw could even fire the shotgun. He was hit and pitched forward. Curly Bob took aim to finish him off.

Kyle drew his Colt revolver and fired, blowing Curly Bob away. The other three gunmen sitting at the table drew their guns and fired at Kyle. The crowd around him had hit the floor. Kyle ducked down and fired back, hitting one of gunmen. Tom Shaw rolled over on the floor in pain. He brought up the shotgun and fired. The second gunman was blown back over a table.

Up on the second floor landing, Paul Taggart took aim on Shaw, who writhed on the floor. Doc Holliday drew the gun from the small of his back and fired. Taggart took the bullet in his shoulder and tumbled down the staircase.

Skeeter stood up. Near her, Kyle had turned toward the staircase, his gun still smoking in his hand. From where Skeeter was standing, it looked as if Kyle was the one who had shot Taggart. Skeeter turned to look at Doc, whose gun was out of sight again. It did not appear as if he was even armed. Tears flooded Skeeter's eyes as she looked at Doc, betrayed.

From behind the bar the third gunman flipped up his table, firing on Kyle. Deke brought up a shotgun from behind the bar and fired both barrels, hitting the third gunman in the back.

Then there was only silence in the Crystal Palace Saloon.

Cordite drifted through the smoke. Tom Shaw lay on the floor in agony. Curly Bob and the three gunmen were dead. Paul Taggart got to his feet at the bottom of the stairs and pushed through the side door out of the saloon. Skeeter ran to her father's side. Homer was with her. Townspeople began to crowd around them.

Outside the Crystal Palace Saloon, Paul Taggart had been winged by Doc's bullet, but his shoulder wound was superficial. Wendell Trask exited the freight office in time to see him. Blackjack Shackleton rode up on a stolen horse. Trask ran over to him. He was stuffing the blueprints he had copied of the *Iron Maiden Stagecoach* into his pocket.

"Got what we needed," Trask told him. "When did you leave Rachel's place?"

"When I saw she had a visitor," Shackleton said.

"Can you ride?"

"I can ride."

Trask grabbed his horse from the hitching post and climbed into the saddle. At that moment Taggart ran out into the street. Shackleton motioned to Trask.

"Pick him up!"

They rode down the street. Kyle exited through the front doors of the Crystal Palace Saloon in time to see Trask pull the wounded Taggart up onto the back of his horse. He and Shackleton galloped past. Shackleton fired on Kyle, who dove to the ground. Once they disappeared Kyle ran to his horse, mounted up and rode after them.

At Rachel's house, the riders stopped. Trask jumped down from the stolen horse and mounted his own horse that was still tied up outside.

Kyle was right behind them.

"Split up!" Skackleton shouted. "Go to the cabin. We will meet you there."

Trask rode off in one direction. Shackleton and Taggart rode in another direction.

In Retribution, Rachel rode up and quickly dismounted, hurrying into the Crystal Palace Saloon. The townspeople cleared a path for her. Skeeter and Homer knelt beside Tom Shaw. Doc Holliday knelt beside them. Shaw's eyes were closed, but he was conscious.

"He's still breathing," Doc said.

"No thanks to you," Skeeter said, fiercely.

Rachel examined Shaw. Up at the bar, Deke Reneker put away the shotgun. Plank joined him. "Drag the bodies out onto the street," Deke murmured. "Let the undertaker know he's working late tonight. Tell the girls to circulate." He raised his voice. "Drinks are on the house for the next twenty minutes!"

There was a rush to the bar from the saloon diehards. The townspeople started to move out. The show was over. They were muted. No one was talking. There was nothing glamorous in this death scene.

Skeeter held her father's hand tightly. Tears streamed down her face. Alice Shaw knelt down on the other side of him. She was ashen and trembling.

She said: "Tom" very softly.

Shaw reached up a bloodstained hand and gripped her arm. His eyes opened for a moment and the smallest of smiles touched his lips.

"Just like it happened in Deadwood…" he said.

Doc straightened. There was nothing he could do for the sheriff. Skeeter averted her eyes, unable to look at him. Doc walked away. The piano player started to pound out a new tune.

Out on the canyon road, thunder rolled again. The air was heavy with the threat of the storm. Shackleton, Taggart and Trask pulled up on their horses.

"You all right?" Trask asked Shackleton.

"Yeah," he said. He looked at Taggart. "How about you?"

"Bullet went right through," Taggart said. "Sore as hell, but the bleeding stopped."

"Kyle Bascomb was at Rachel's place," Shackleton said. "He was in the posse who shot up the picnic and murdered all those innocent folks. I will never forget his face. Maybe he was visiting the doctor. I fired on him on the porch, but I missed him. But he is in my sights now."

"That might have been him in town riding out after us," Trask said.

He took a pair of binoculars from a leather pouch and put them to his eyes.Through them he could see Kyle's figure, on horseback, pretty far back, a silhouette against the moonlight. Trask lowered the binoculars.

"He's still with us," he said. "Do we go back and try to pick him off?"

"It is enough that I have seen him again," Shackleton said. "There will another time for us to catch up with him. Let us put some distance between him and us."

They rode on.

Outside the Crystal Palace Saloon, Otis Larchmont hoisted Sheriff Shaw up onto the back of a buckboard with Rachel. A few spectators watched, Deke and Missy Vartan among them. Skeeter and Homer stood to one side. Missy nodded at Skeeter.

"Who is that with Homer?"

"I believe her name is Abigail, but everyone in town calls her Skeeter," Deke Reneker said. "She is the sheriff's daughter. The family's been here about eight months."

"Homer and Skeeter seem close," Missy said.

"Homer doesn't go anywhere without her," Deke said, mockingly.

At the buckboard Alice held onto her husband's hand until the last possible moment.

"Gotta get him to my place, Mrs. Shaw," Rachel said, gently. She turned to Otis Larchmont. "I need to examine your head wound."

Otis looked around at the townspeople watching, as if embarrassed. "One of them hit me from behind."

"Did you get a look at the person?" Deke asked.

"He was just a shadow."

"We need to go," Rachel said, urgently.

Otis nodded and pulled himself into the back of the buckboard. Rachel took the reins. The buckboard pulled away from the Crystal Palace Saloon. The crowd broke up around Skeeter and Homer, heading back to the town hall party. Skeeter watched the buckboard driving away. Missy Vartan looked at the bright windows of the Crystal Palace Saloon.

"Six men were gunned down in your saloon and that doesn't appear to have hurt your business," she said.

"It never does," Deke said, almost cheerfully.

"The outlaws were all inside the saloon," Missy said. "So who could have knocked out Deputy Larchmont? It certainly made for a more spectacular show if the sheriff was forced to face these outlaws alone."

Deke's voice was like ice now. "It did, didn't it?"

"You had no hand in that?"

"None whatsoever. May I escort you back to your party?"

Missy looked at him for a long moment, then nodded and took his arm.

On the lonely stretch of road, ragged clouds raced across the moon. Thunder cracked directly overhead. The light rain became a downpour. Shackleton, Trask and Taggart pulled up their horses. Shackleton looked behind them.

"That marshal's gaining on us."

"Let us see if I can slow him down some," Trask said.

He removed something from a leather pouch, then pulled his rifle out of its scabbard. He affixed a modified spyglass into a groove that he had rigged on the top of the rifle.

"What is that?" Taggart asked.

"It's how we're gonna take that Iron Maiden gold shipment," Trask replied. "Might as well give it a trial run."

He put the rifle to his shoulder and peered through the magnified sight. Kyle could be seen riding through the trees. Rain distorted his figure. He came into sharper focus, but he was still only a silhouetted shape.

It would take a marksman's shot.

Shackleton shook his head. "You're too far away."

"Not with this rifle," Trask said.

"How long have you been carrying it?"

"A few weeks. Had it delivered just before the wedding party. It has a telescopic sight on it. A magnification factor of ten and produces an image ten times closer to the object."

Trask fired the rifle. Kyle pitched off his horse in the forest and sprawled onto the ground. He lay motionless. Trask lowered the rifle.

"Pretty accurate shot," Taggart said. "Did you kill him?"

"Can't tell from this distance," Trask said.

"I got my revenge," Shackleton said. "Leave him to the wolves. We need fresh mounts."

The three outlaws wheeled their horses around in the downpour and rode on.

8

Pocket Watch

Rain lashed Rachel's house. In the front room, Otis Larchmont paced restlessly. There was a bandage on the side of his head, the dried blood washed from his face. Alice Shaw sat with her hands folded in her lap. Her hands were trembling. Mayor Ballantyne hovered near the doorway, restless to leave. Rachel had been tending to Sheriff Shaw. Now she entered the front room.

"Your husband is resting now, Alice," she said. "The bullet missed a major artery by a couple of inches. I got it out. Best if he is not moved. I will monitor him throughout the night."

"Is he going to live?" Alice asked in a whisper.

"If he makes it to sunrise, he's got a very good chance," Rachel said.

Mayor Ballantyne turned to Otis. "You're the acting sheriff now, Otis."

Otis was startled. "I can't accept that offer," he protested.

"I am exercising the profundity of my office and decreeing you the position." The mayor turned to Alice. "Just until your husband is up on his feet again, Mrs.

Shaw. Which, God willing, will be very soon. Good work, Doctor. The entire town is in your debt."

Otis helped Alice to her feet. It was like she was in a daze. They moved out into the driving rain. Rachel closed the door. She moved back into the front room.

Shackleton's gun belt was thrown onto a table.

Rachel jumped. Deke Reneker emerged from the shadows. Rachel held her ground. "What are you doing here?"

"Just a friendly visit," Deke said, evenly. "I guess the sheriff isn't the only man you dug a bullet out of tonight, Rachel."

"What makes you say that?"

"Call it a hunch. I figured where Shackleton's men are their boss cannot be far away. He must have left in a hurry not to take his gun belt. What shape is he in?"

Rachel's attitude toward Deke was guarded. "He'll live."

"It seems like you traded one patient for another. Blackjack Shackleton for Sheriff Tom Shaw. Quite a night for you."

"You gonna keep my secret?" Rachel asked.

"That you attended to a notorious outlaw wanted in connection to crimes in two States?" Deke shrugged and smiled. "Of course. Let me know if Sheriff Shaw lives or dies."

"Do you care?"

Deke looked at her as if thoughtful. "Actually, I do."

He left the house by the front door.

Kyle Bascomb came to consciousness on the ground with the rain sweeping over him like a shroud. He sat up, pain throbbing through his body. The bullet from Trask's gun had ceased his forehead. He lay there, wondering if the outlaws were going to come back to finish him off. There were small sounds all around him, scurrying animals in the underbrush, but the Shackleton gang did not return. Kyle got to his feet and found his horse grazing among the trees. He pulled himself up into the saddle and rode off.

Inside the Crystal Palace Saloon, Deke Reneker was silhouetted in the doorway of his second floor balcony. A sound swung him around, the small derringer in his sleeve falling into his right hand. Missy Vartan stood in a cobweb of shadows. Deke returned the derringer to its hiding place. Missy stepped forward.

"Have you got any word of the sheriff's condition?"

"I left Tom Shaw in Dr. Rachel Drake's capable hands. She can work miracles. I will look in on him in the morning. I thought by now you were suffering more of Mayor Ballantyne's outlandish stories about life in a frontier town."

Missy moved toward him. "I have heard them all. This is the twelfth stop on my so-called 'world tour'. Next I am scheduled to play in St. Louis, Dodge City, Abilene, St. Joseph, Fort Laramie, Virginia City and Santa Fe. I could have skipped the booking in Retribution, but I knew I had to come back and face my demons."

Deke poured them each a glass of champagne and handed one of them to Missy. "What demons would they be?"

"Confronting my past." Missy sipped at the champagne, then set down her glass, moving closer to Deke. "For the longest time I held you responsible for ruining my life."

"There may be some truth to that," Deke allowed, quietly.

"There isn't. I made my own way in the world and everything that has happened to me has been calculated. You saw to that. You groomed me for the theater for as long as I can remember. I did not know how I would react to seeing you again. Now I know. It was the reason I came back to Retribution."

"And what reason was that?"

"To tell you that I never hated you," Missy said, quietly. "I was grateful to you. You have been good to the people in this town."

Deke was touched by her words. "You are in a very small minority."

"People here know you are ruthless and expedient," Missy said. "You hold markers on the folks here that can be cashed in. But they also know you've got a good heart."

"They are mistaken," Deke said.

Missy shook her head. "I don't think so."

She moved into his arms and kissed him. Their kiss and embrace became passionate.

Outside the rain continued to lacerate Saratoga Street.

Kyle rode through the forest. He could see a ranch through the trees. The rain was even heavier now. There was no sign of anyone. Kyle rode up to the barn, dismounted and drew his gun. A dread had suddenly come over him. He knew the Blaisdell family by sight, but that was all.

He found Tom Blaisdell and his two teenage sons in the front yard. They had been shot. With his heart hammering in his chest, Kyle approached the Blaisdell house. The front door was ajar. He pulled it all the way open. Inside he found Sarah Blaisdell lying on the floor of the front room. She had been raped and beaten, but something had

interrupted her attackers. They had left her barely cling-
ing to life. Kyle went out to the barn, unhooked the water
canteen from his saddle and moved back into the house.
Gently he lifted the water to Sarah's lips. She nodded, sipping a little. Kyle lifted her up into his arms. She was an
attractive woman in her late forties with dark hair with
little ringlets woven into it. Her dress had been ripped
open and Kyle brought the fabric together so that it covered her breasts. She looked up at him a little dazed, as if
she were not sure where she was.

"I knew your husband and son," Kyle said. "I don't
know your name."

"Sarah Blaisdell," she murmured. Her voice was a
husky rasp. "They came into the house asking for direc-
tions to Retribution. I told them that it was about twenty
miles from our place. I invited them in for coffee. All the
time I talked to them, my husband and my sons were lying dead in the front yard."

Kyle lifted her up a little bit more. "Who did this to
you?"

"I did not know them," Sarah Blaisdell said. "Strangers. One of them had a shoulder wound. The other had a
more serious wound which had been bandaged up. But
that did not stop the big man from throwing me down to
the floor. He ripped at my clothes. I tried to fight him off,
but he was too strong. When he was finished with me he
left me on the kitchen floor. One of the younger men was
going to kill me, but the other man said just to leave me.
I did not hear anything more. The other man said they
needed to hurry. I heard them ride away." She looked up
into Kyle's face. "Who were they?"

"John Shackleton and three members of his outlaw
gang," Kyle said. "I have been tracking them. I'm going to
get you to a doctor."

Sarah Blaisdell shook her head. "Too late for that." She reached up, grasping Kyle's arm. "The wounded man had a gold pocket watch. It looked very old. An antique. When he threw me down to the floor the gold chain broke. I do not even know if he was aware of losing it. I picked it up and slid it under the stove. Right there."

Kyle looked, but he did not see it.

At that moment Sarah Blaisdell gave a little shudder and slumped down into Kyle's arms. She was dead. Kyle allowed the moment of grief to wash over him. He leaned down on his hands and knees and pulled out an ornate gold pocket watch from beneath the stove. He got to his feet and turned it over in his hands.

The initials 'JS" were engraved on it.

Kyle knew immediately who the initials stood for.
John Shackleton.

Kyle did not think that Shackleton was even aware that he had lost it here in the Blaisdell house. It would be too far for him to return. Kyle's thumb flipped the pocket watch open. It played a soft, melodious tune. Kyle thought it was *Greensleeves.* Inside were two small pictures of a man and a woman, obviously Shackleton's parents, cracked and yellowed with age. Kyle straightened, putting the pocket watch into his coat pocket, looking down sadly at Sarah Blaisdell.

He had a personal score to settle now with Shackleton.

It took Kyle an hour to bury the four members of the Blaisdell family beneath a flowing cheery tree. He fashioned four crude crosses with materials he found in the barn. Kyle was not much for praying, but he *did* say a prayer for the Blaisdells. He climbed onto his horse. He had no idea where the outlaws had gone. The trail was cold.

Kyle turned back toward Retribution.

At the Shaw house the next day the storm was still raging. Paintings were off the walls, kitchen items and keepsakes off the shelves and mantlepiece. Alice was packing everything into boxes. It looked as if she had been at it all night. Her eyes were hollow with exhaustion. There was no sign of Skeeter.

In the Crystal Palace Saloon Deke Reneker stood at his open balcony drinking a cup of coffee. Missy came up behind him wearing a silk robe. She rested her head against his arm.

"Would you believe me if I told you I still loved you?" she asked him.

"That would warm my heart, but I know you won't be staying," Deke said. "You have got other towns to delight and enthrall."

Below they could see Homer walking down the opposite boardwalk. He was looking for Skeeter.

"It would be a sad thing if the Shaw family leaves," Missy said. "Retribution needs a good schoolteacher."

"Whether her husband lives or dies, she won't stay," Deke said.

"Homer will be lost without Skeeter."

"He'll get over it."

"But will he? I'm not so sure of that."

"They are childhood friends. Once Skeeter is gone, Homer will find new friends."

"Not easily."

"He will cope." Deke took another swallow of coffee. "All children do."

There was a moment's pause while Missy looked at him. Then she said: "Homer does not know that I am his *real* mother?"

Deke stared out into the awakening Retribution street. "He does not."

"What was the story you put into his mind about his real mother?"

Deke shrugged. "I told him she had died in childbirth."

Missy laid her head against Deke's shoulder. She said softly: "She did."

Kyle entered Rachel's house after he returned from the Blaisdell place. Rachel moved into his arms and gingerly touched the bullet crease along his forehead.

"You're hurt."

"I am fine. What has happened to Tom Shaw?"

"He is sleeping right now. Did you catch up with the outlaws?"

"Not yet," he said. "But I aim to. You all right?"

"I'm tired. It has been a long night."

"What are Sheriff Shaw's chances for survival?"

"Fifty-fifty," Rachel said. "His wife was practically catatonic when she was here. His daughter Skeeter feels betrayed by your friend Doc Holliday. He wounded one of Shackleton's outlaws, but apparently Skeeter did not see that. There is no one for her to trust anymore."

"I'll deal with that situation," Kyle said. "Let me know about the sheriff's condition."

He moved out of her arms to the front door.

"Are you staying in Retribution?" she asked him.

"I am until you give me your answer whether you have decided to leave with me or not."

"I need time to answer your question," Rachel said, softly.

"I will give you all the time you need," Kyle said.

Rachel watched him leave, her emotions clearly torn.

Rain continued to sweep across streets of Retribution. Most of the people had been driven inside by the deluge. Kyle untied his horse at the front of the livery stable and crossed the street toward Elliott's Breakfast Emporium around the corner. Skeeter ran out into the downpour. For once Homer was not tagging behind her. She grabbed Kyle's arm.

"Marshal! I looked all over for you last night! I wanted to thank you for saving my father's life."

"He did real good on his own," Kyle said.

They walked together along the boardwalk.

"He didn't see that back-shooter on the stairs in the Crystal Palace Saloon last night," Skeeter said. "But *you* did!"

"I stopped by Dr. Drake's place this morning," Kyle said. "Your father is doing well. He is sleeping right now."

"The Doc says it ain't a sure thing. But he is gonna pull through. I know he will! I am going over to the doctor's place as soon as I can."

Kyle glanced around. "Where is your better half?"

"If you mean that good-for nothin' ruffian rat, Homer is in the saloon tending to his chores for his father. I think that Songbird of Europe and the Americas is with him. Deke Reneker makes my skin itch, but I guess he is sweet on her." They walked further down the boardwalk. "How come you ain't the marshal here in Retribution?"

"Going to hand my badge to your father when he recovers from his wounds."

"You're the best, Marshal!" Skeeter said. "If it came to a shootout between you and that cowardly Doc Holliday, I know who would pull leather faster."

"Sometimes people do things their own way, Skeeter," Kyle told her, kindly.

"Doc didn't even have a gun at the saloon last night!" Skeeter exclaimed.

"He had one," Kyle corrected her. "He just made sure no one saw it."

Skeeter stopped in her tracks. She clutched Kyle's arm. "What are you sayin'?"

"That I didn't shoot that outlaw Wendell Trask off that balcony in the Crystal Place Saloon," Kyle said. "I didn't even see him up there. But Doc did. By the time you looked over, his gun was back under his coat. That was the way he wanted it."

Skeeter was stunned by the revelation. Her eyes filled with tears. "I gotta go now, Marshal!"

She ran off. Kyle headed on to Elliott's Breakfast Emporium.

Skeeter came to a skidding stop outside Doc Holliday's cottage. The curtains at the windows were pulled closed. Skeeter tried the front door. It was unlocked. She crept inside. It might as well have been night. The only illumination came from a Tiffany lamp on a desk. Doc sat in his front room. There were two nickel-plated revolvers on the desk, along with a bottle of whiskey and a bloodstained handkerchief. Also a telegram that was open beside his right hand. He coughed rackingly. When he looked down there was blood on the handkerchief. Skeeter moved through the overlapping shadows up to Doc. She was suddenly frightened. "Doc? Are you sick?"

Doc Holliday turned in the chair, grabbing one of the nickel-plated revolvers. Then he saw who it was and relaxed. He slumped back, setting the revolver down on the desk. His voice was hoarse.

"Go home, Skeeter."

"Let me get Dr. Drake," Skeeter pleaded. "She'll fix you up real good."

"There is nothing that she can do for me that has not been done already."

Skeeter moved closer. She noticed the telegram open on the desk. It said: "*Need you in Tombstone*." And it was signed: "*Wyatt Earp*".

"Are you going to Tombstone, Doc?" Skeeter asked him.

"My travel plans have not been finalized. Whatever they are, they have nothing to do with you."

"Doc, I'm sorry," she said, and her voice was hushed. "Marshal Bascomb told me what happened at the Crystal Palace last night. You shot that cowardly backshooter who had drawn on you. I had no call to wail on you the way I did."

Doc had another coughing fit. Skeeter waited until it had passed.

"Now that my integrity has been reinstated in your eyes," he murmured, "you can do me the kindness of going away."

Skeeter looked from him to the open telegram and back. "Why does Wyatt Earp need you?"

"That is not any of your business," Doc said. "You been doggin' my footsteps for too long. Leave me in peace now."

"But Doc---"

"Get out of here!" he said, roughly.

Skeeter scuttled away back into the shadows. A moment later the front door slammed. Doc took another swig of whiskey, then got to his feet. He put the two revolvers into his waistband, shrugged on a long gray coat and stuffed the telegram into the pocket of his waistcoat. He picked up his ornate walking cane.

Outside in the street, Skeeter did not know what to do. She was of a mind to ride out to see her father at Rachel's place but, once she had done that, there was nothing else for her do right now. She looked around for Homer, but there was no sign of him in the street. She could roust Marshal Bascomb from his meal at Elliot's Breakfast Emporium, but he would likely just give her another lecture about how she should stay away from Doc Holliday. She knew that Doc did not want her getting under his feet and being a bother to him. But she felt the need to look out for him, even though she knew that would not sit well with him.

On a whim, she ran to the back gate to Doc's patio and saw Doc Holliday, aided by his cane, walking down Chestnut Street before turning the corner onto Saratoga Street. Skeeter followed him at a respectable distance until he moved into the Retribution livery stable. She had no idea where Doc was headed, but somehow she knew it was important. Doc Holliday never left his house unless there was a very good reason. Skeeter ran down to where her horse was grazing outside her two-story house. She caught a glimpse of her mother in the front room windows. She looked as if she was packing some boxes. Skeeter untied her horse, a small roan, and climbed up onto it. She took a circuitous route which brought her to the Retribution livery stable in time to see Doc Holliday ride away down Saratoga Street on his way out of town.

Skeeter followed Doc, leaving a respectable distance between them as they rode out of town.

The town of Kettleberg was a muddier, more run-down version of Retribution, with saloons, a barber shop, a livery stable, two rooming houses, a freight office and a Chinese section of the town. Their "tent city" encroached right onto the main street. The Iron Maiden stood outside the Kettleberg Freight Office. It looked exactly like the graphic design from the blueprints in Hoss Cavanaugh's office. Steel plates had been welded onto the stagecoach chassis. There were holes for rifle barrels on both sides of the coach. The only way into the armored vehicle was from the top, where a hatch could be pulled up. There was the usual platform for a driver and a guard.

Hoss Cavanaugh stood with the Kettleberg marshal, a big man named McClarnon who sported a drooping moustache, bushy sideburns, had quick, bright eyes and a Southern drawl. He patted the Iron Maiden stagecoach.

"She's a beauty," the marshal said. "I didn't think you would be ready in time."

"It took some work on the steel plates," Hoss said, "and we drilled more holes for the rifle barrels. The Iron Maiden can accommodate two marshals, two inside and two more on the outside. No one is going to try to hold up the Iron Maiden while I am riding on it!"

"When do you take the gold shipment?" McClarnon asked.

"Two days," Hoss said.

"Where are you headed?"

"That's a secret. No one knows the route but me." He grinned. "No one's getting this shipment, Marshal!"

Dense trees surrounded a log cabin in the woodlands. Inside, Paul Taggart was redressing Shackleton's wound, which had started bleeding again. He wrapped tape tightly around the injury. Wendell Trask entered the cabin. Shackleton looked at him, setting his .45 revolver back down beside him.

"What's the word?"

"The Iron Maiden's gonna leave Kettleberg day after tomorrow," Trask said.

"And nobody knows it has been delivered?"

"Only the sheriff in Kettleberg, fellah named McClarnon. Hoss Cavanaugh has been going through the Iron Maiden making sure it all checks out. I will be staying in Kettleberg at the Silver Dollar Saloon. Hoss has never seen me there. I will be sure he leaves Kettleberg on time."

"Good enough," Shackleton said, pain making his emotions ragged.

"Did you find Marshal Bascomb's body?" Taggart asked.

"I looked for it on the way back here," Trask said. "There was no sign of it. Either the marshal crawled away to die, or somehow he got back to his feet and rode away. I didn't feel like going back into Retribution to find out."

"Whether the marshal is living or not makes no difference to me," Taggart said. "He won't be tracking us either way."

"I did hear some news in Fargo Springs," Trask said. "Kyle Bascomb tangled with Jefferson Forrester who had been leading that posse when they hit us at the church. The way I heard it, Bascomb shot Forrester stone cold dead in a hotel room where he was entertaining some ladies of the night. So you got some revenge back on that posse, Blackjack."

"I am glad to hear that," Shackleton said, softly. "But if Marshal Bascomb is still alive, my account with him won't be settled until I put him in the ground."

9

OK Corral

TOMBSTONE WAS A SPRAWLING frontier town that had mushroomed to fourteen thousand souls. Skeeter rode into the east side of the town, looking at the buildings with some awe. There was a bowling alley, four churches, an ice-house, a school, two banks, three newspapers, an ice cream parlor and Skeeter lost count how many saloons, gambling establishments and brothels there were. She tied her roan up outside the Alhambra Saloon. The streets of Tombstone were virtually empty. She found her way to Allen Street where she spied Doc Holliday's horse tied up outside the livery stable. She looked up at the Long Branch Saloon and ventured inside, but there was no sign of Doc Holliday. In fact, the saloon was also practically deserted.

Skeeter moved to the swing doors of the saloon and resolved to wait for Doc.

Doc Holliday climbed the stairs of the Opulent Grand Hotel to the second floor. He walked down the corridor to the corner room and opened the door. Wyatt Earp whirled, his Buntline .45 Colt Revolver in his right hand, then relaxed when he saw who it was. Doc moved over to a table where a bottle of whiskey stood. He helped himself to a shot and moved to the window overlooking Allen Street. He noted the Marshal's badge on Wyatt's waistcoat.

"Didn't know if you were going to make it in time, Doc," Wyatt said.

"Your telegram was ambiguous," he said, "but intriguing. Where did you get the long handgun?"

Wyatt holstered the 12-inch barrel revolver. "Ned Buntline made it specially for me."

"Good balance?"

"The best."

Wyatt took out a shotgun out of the wardrobe.

"You're a United States Marshal now?" Doc asked him.

"That's right," Wyatt said. "So are my brothers Virgil and Morgan."

"So this is a family affair?"

Wyatt looked over at him. "Ike Clayton, the McLaurys and Billy Claiborne have called me out. They have been threatening my family for weeks. They are waiting for us at the OK Corral. But this does not have to be your fight, Doc."

"Are you going to deputize me?"

"For this one time only. If you will allow for that."

Doc nodded. "I will." He finished up the whiskey and turned from the window. "I see your brothers are already waiting out there."

Doc suffered a coughing spell and waited for it to pass. He was pale and his hands shook a little. Wyatt watched him carefully. "You going to be all right?"

"Never better," Doc said.

Wyatt threw the shotgun to Doc. The two of them moved from the suite out into the corridor and down the stairs of the Grand Hotel.

Outside on Allen Street, Skeeter watched as Wyatt Earp and Doc Holliday emerged from the Grand Hotel. Both of them wore Marshal's badges. Doc carried his walking cane, but he did not lean on it heavily. His breathing was still labored. Skeeter could see that he was very pale. She followed a good distance behind him.

Wyatt Earp and Doc Holliday climbed up on the boardwalk in front of the Alhambra Saloon where Wyatt's brother Virgil Earp was waiting. He was wearing a long black duster, his Marshal badge pinned to his waistcoat. Morgan Earp had exited the Alhambra Saloon, also wearing a long black duster and a Marshal's badge and walked over quickly to them.

"Ike Clayton has taken a position in front of the OK Corral," Virgil said.

"His brother Billy is with him," Morgan said. "They have Tom and Frank McLaury backing them up."

"What about Billy Claiborne?" Wyatt asked.

"He's with them," Virgil said. "He was at the Alhambra Saloon until a few minutes ago."

"So that is all of them," Morgan said. "Ike won't bring any more men with them."

"This is personal fight," Wyatt said. "They have been biding their time, waiting for the right moment. They want to finish it." He nodded at Doc. "You both know Doc Holliday."

"This ain't your fight, Doc," Virgil said.

"Wyatt is my friend," Doc said, simply. "Besides, he has deputized me. Makes it a special occasion."

"This the way you are calling it, Wyatt?" Morgan asked.

"It is."

"John Plum and the Tombstone Vigilance Committee are behind us," Virgil said, "but we don't want no civilians getting killed."

"Look to the streets," Wyatt advised. "Folks are getting out of our way."

The Earp brothers looked around.

Allen Street was eerily deserted.

Skeeter had taken shelter in the alleyway across the street. It was in shadows, leaving her to peer out at Allen Street like a wraith. On the boardwalk, the Earps were talking quietly, their voices not quite carrying to where Skeeter had hidden herself. Wind whipped at the marshals' long duster coats. Thunder rolled distantly. More doors were closing along Allen Street as the atmosphere took a heady turn. The lawmen were acutely aware that people's lives could be on the line. They all had handguns, including Wyatt who carried his Colt Buntline Special.

The Earps and Doc Holliday stepped off the boardwalk outside the Alhambra Saloon and walked slowly down the street. Those folks who were in the doorways of the saloons and outside the Tombstone *Epitaph* newspaper watched as the Earps headed toward the OK Corral.

A growing sense of violence wrapped itself around them.

Skeeter ventured out of her hiding place in the alleyway off Allen Street and followed the lawmen at a safe distance. She doubted the Earps would not know her if they fell over her, but Doc Holliday would not take it kindly to her putting herself in harm's way. She kept a respectable distance from the lawmen, finding doorways and alleyways to scuttle into as she made her way along the boardwalk.

The Earps walked down Third Street which connected to Fremont Street. Skeeter noted an elegantly dressed man hustle up to the Earps. She did not know his name, but he was wearing a Sheriff's badge on his fancy waistcoat. Then she heard his name was *Johnny Behan.*

"There are no firearms allowed in Tombstone, Wyatt," Behan said, pleasantly, but the tension was evident in his voice. "That means no Bowie knives, dirks, pistols and rifles may be carried on the streets. Hand over your weapons."

"I don't believe we will do that today, Sheriff," Wyatt said.

Behan's affable façade was fading fast. "Then it is my sworn duty to disarm you."

"We don't have time for this," Virgil Earp said.

"Stand aside, Behan," Morgan said.

The Earps left the sheriff standing in the dust in the middle of Third Street.

Skeeter dashed down the alleyway and pulled up to see the Earps and Doc Holliday turn back onto Fremont Street. A building there was under construction. Opposite it was a narrow alleyway that backed up onto the OK Corral. Skeeter noted that *C.S. Fly's Boarding House and Photographic Studio* was on one side.

The lawmen approached the OK Corral. True to her nickname, Skeeter scooted ahead of them and hid in the skeletal framework of the building that was still under construction.

Most of what happened next was seen from Skeeter's perspective.

Ike Clanton was trying to sober up, pouring a bucket of water over his head. Near him were Billy Clanton, Tom McLaury, Frank McLaury and Billy Clairborne. All of them were armed with Colt .45 Revolvers.

The Earps and Doc Holliday turned down into the alley outside the OK Corral.

The cowboys fanned out in front of them.

Virgil raised his voice. "We're here to disarm you! Throw up your hands!"

Billy Clanton and Frank McLaury reached for the revolvers in their belts.

"Hold on!" Virgil said. "I don't want that!"

Billy Claiborne ran away through an open gate. Billy Clanton and Frank McLaury drew their revolvers. Wyatt Earp drew his Buntline Special. Billy Clanton got off the first shot, but he missed Wyatt. Wyatt shot Frank McLaury. Doc fired the double-barreled shotgun at Tom McLaury, who fired his revolver. He was hit. Doc blasted the second barrel of the shotgun at him and tossed the shotgun aside, drawing his revolvers. Virgil and Morgan Earp fired on Frank McLaury and Billy Clanton. Ike Clanton ran toward Wyatt, his arms held high.

"Don't shoot me!" Ike pleaded. "I got no gun! I got no gun!"

He grabbed hold of Wyatt, who hurled him to one side. "Go to fighting or get away!"

Clanton stumbled down Fremont Street.

Skeeter saw it all from her vantage point in the skeletal building under construction. Her overriding emotion was for Doc. Virgil, Morgan and Wyatt Earp kept firing on Frank McLaury and Billy Clanton. Frank McLaury shot Virgil Earp in the calf, sending him to the ground in agony. Billy Clanton shot Morgan Earp in the chest.

Doc and Wyatt Earp shot Billy Clanton numerous times

Doc ran out of bullets in one of his guns. Frank McLaury took aim on him.

"I got you now, you son of a bitch!" McLaury shouted.

A small smile tugged at Doc's lips. "You're my Huckleberry if you do."

Doc shot him with his second revolver. Morgan Earp shot him again. McLaury was thrown back to the muddy ground. Immediately, Doc leaned over with a coughing spell that lasted several seconds.

Drifting cordite and silence prevailed in the OK Corral.

From start to finish, the whole gunfight had taken just under thirty seconds.

Skeeter edged forward, making sure that Doc was still standing. A crowd of townspeople had gathered. Sheriff Behan emerged from Fly's Photographic Studio, moving toward Wyatt. He was acutely aware of the townspeople watching. With a grandiose gesture, playing to the crowd, he called out: "All of you are under arrest!"

Wyatt turned to him. "I don't think I'll let you arrest us today, Behan."

Doc suddenly turned around, staring at the building under construction outside the OK Corral. He thought he caught a glimpse of what looked like a tomboy fleeing the scene of the gunfire.

Virgil and Morgan's wives ran up, completely distraught. Wyatt helped Virgil and Morgan to their feet. Both of them were wounded, but their injuries were not life-threatening. Doc turned back and looked down at the dead men outside the OK Corral.

"Hell of a thing," he said.

Skeeter had reached her horse where it was tied up on Allen Street and climbed up into the saddle. More townspeople were heading in the direction of the gunfight. Doc Holliday had broken away from the Earps and leaned on his cane. In the distance he could just make out Skeeter's slight figure galloping away from Allen Street before she turned the corner onto Second Street. There was an unruly mob forming around the bodies of the dead men. Wyatt detached himself away from the mayhem and walked over to Doc. He followed his gaze.

"Who is that riding away from Allen Street?"

"My shadow," Doc said, ironically.

Wyatt turned as Johnny Behan thrust his way toward them.

"Better get our stories straight," Wyatt said.

Doc nodded. "Better had."

Skeeter galloped down Fremont Street away from the gunfight.

But she knew Doc Holliday had seen her.

Missy Vartan had no idea why she had come to the Musical Hall Theater in Retribution in the middle of the day. Her performance had been a rousing success and she had graciously accepted the mayor's offer to stay one more night for an encore performance. She had enjoyed her time in Retribution. She was scheduled to leave the next day on the stage to Virginia City. She looked around in the shadows, noting again that the ceiling was decimated with several bullet holes denoting the rapture with which the cowboys celebrated the various performances. The theater in St. Louis was a much grander affair with tiered seating and two balconies. But Missy Vartan had grown up here in Retribution and for her the Musical Hall Theater had a lot of memories.

She was aware that she was not alone in the shrouded theater. The sound of quiet crying reached her. She walked down one of the aisles to find Homer Reneker sitting in the first row. The gaudy backdrop of a New York City street scene hung down from the stage. Missy gently put her hand on Homer's shoulder. He immediately cowered away from her, embarrassed that he had been caught crying.

"It's Homer, isn't it?" Missy said, softly.

Homer snuffled back his tears. "Yes, ma'am. I was not crying. Sometimes I get all choked up with feelings that will not go away. My friend Skeeter says it is because I have my head in the clouds all day so I cannot see the rainbows."

"Your friend Skeeter sounds like a very special friend," Missy said.

"Yeah, she is, but she ain't been around for a while. Her ma is packing up their house. Her husband is the sheriff, Tom Shaw, but he got shot last night. Skeeter says he is going to be all right."

"I am happy to hear that."

"It will not be the same for me if she leaves," Homer said.

"Maybe she will stay right here in Retribution. A friend like that is a treasure you should always cherish."

"Yeah, I know that, but mostly she is ragging on me for something I done. You have a friend like that? Someone you look up to, but you cannot hold onto?"

"Yes, I have a friend like that," Missy said, wistfully. "He doesn't believe he is a good man, but he is."

"My pa is Deke Reneker," Homer said.

"Is that right?"

"Folks in town are afraid of him, but they shouldn't be. Are you going to stay in Retribution?"

"I have one more performance to give, then I will be leaving on the stage tomorrow morning."

"Be sure to come by and say goodbye," Homer said.

He fled up the aisle to the front of the Music Hall stage and disappeared. Missy choked back some tears of her own, not that Homer would have known that.

But she had been thankful for the opportunity to visit with her son.

Skeeter rode back to Retribution and tied her horse in some oak trees at the back of her house. She entered the house to find it in darkness, light being held back by the curtains. Alice Shaw sat alone in an armchair, more open boxes around her, staring into the shadows. There was a bottle of laudanum on a table beside her. Skeeter knelt down next to the chair and took her mother's hand. Alice looked at her and her voice was a little dreamy.

"Skeeter. I have not seen you in the house."

"I had some errands to attend to," Skeeter said, gently. "I'm here now, Ma. I will not leave you alone again. I will help you with the packing."

"Where is your father? He does not seem to be here."

"He got shot, Mama. You know that. Rachel and Otis Larchmont took him to Rachel's place. She is looking out for him. He is going to be all right. I know he will be."

Alice turned toward her daughter, as if she had just realized that she was there. "No, he is needed in Retribution. He is the sheriff here. He has duties he has to attend to."

"I know that, Ma," Skeeter said, softly. "He is very well liked in the town."

"Such a fine figure of a man," Alice said. "Always dapper and courtly. He is very proud of you, Abigail."

"You never call me Abigail," Skeeter said, her heart breaking. "You always call me Skeeter, Ma. *Always.*"

Alice brushed some hair from Skeeter's face, smoothing it down on her head. "You remember when I would brush your hair when you were a little girl? It was fine then, like spun golden fleece. You let me do that for hours. Never complained."

"I remember, Ma."

Skeeter laid her head down on her mother's lap.

Alice began singing a soft lullaby to her.

10

Iron Maiden

IN ELLIOTT'S BREAKFAST EMPORIUM Kyle sat at a table finishing off a breakfast of steak and eggs. It was a couple days later and the news about the gunfight at the OK Corral was the main topic conversation in the town. Kyle noted that Waco was in a corner table wolfing down eggs and waffles. Kyle knew that Waco worked sometimes for Blackjack Shackleton. Kyle put Shackleton's distinctive pocket watch on his table. He noted Waco taking an interest in it as he ate his breakfast. Kyle opened the pocket watch. *Greensleeves* played softly. He pocketed the watch, got up from the table and exited the restaurant.

He did not have to wait long.

The alleyway between the buildings was filled with shadows. Waco came up behind Kyle, a Bowie knife in his hand. Kyle whirled. He ripped the knife out of Waco's hand and slammed him up against the side of the building. The point of the knife came against Waco's throat.

"Morning, Waco," Kyle said, conversationally. "I had not seen you in Retribution. You got some business here in town?"

"Nothing that would concern you."

"I thought that last magazine article about you gunning three men in Abilene in under thirty seconds was a tad exaggerated."

Waco shrugged. "I don't write them, Marshal."

Kyle eased off him a step, but his hand hovered over the butt of the .45 revolver in his gun belt.

"Still working for Blackjack Shackleton?"

Waco's demeaner was relaxed. He shrugged again. "He pays more money than most."

"That pocket watch I was looking at during breakfast. You seemed to notice it."

"A fine piece," Waco allowed. "Where did you get it?"

"Off the body of a woman named Sarah Blaisdell. She was murdered in her house along with her husband and son. You wouldn't know anything about that?"

"Not a thing. But it is a fancy piece."

"If Blackjack wants his pocket watch back," Kyle said, evenly, "he'll need to come and find me."

"I will be sure to let him know that."

Kyle flipped the Bowie knife and thrust the hilt into Waco's hand. He turned and walked away. Waco went for his gun.

Doc stepped out of the shadows, one of his nickel-plated guns in his hand.

"I hope you're not thinking of doing anything foolish, Waco?"

Waco's hand came off the hilt of his gun. "Mornin', Doc." Kyle's hand hovered near the butt of his revolver. But Waco's attention was on Doc. "I hear you killed some friends of mine in Tombstone. You and the Earps. Tom and Frank McLaury were good people."

"I'm sure they were mourners at their funeral," Doc said.

"You're looking a little peaked, Doc," Waco said. "Guess the experience did not sit right with you."

"The lighting in this alleyway does not do me justice. Out in the sunlight, I am positively pale."

"I hear that Justice Spiar ruled that the Earps and you had been deputized by Virgil Earp," Waco said. "The gunfight was deemed justified within the law. That must have been a weight of your mind."

"It surely was," Doc said.

"Well, I will be on my way," Waco said. He tipped his hat. "Doc." He turned back to Kyle. "Marshal."

Waco moved away. Doc holstered his gun. He and Kyle took a walk down Saratoga Street. A storm was gathering again, the sky dark with black clouds.

"Way I heard it," Kyle said, "the Clantons and the McLaurys had been threatening the Earps for weeks."

"Virgil Earp is the marshal in Tombstone," Doc said. "His brother Morgan is the assistant town marshal. They walked down to the OK Corral to disarm these ruffians. Wyatt and I went along, fully deputized. The cowboys did not wish to give up their weapons."

"Who fired the first shot?" Kyle asked.

"Billy Clanton."

"I hear the gunfight took all of thirty seconds."

"Was it that long?" Doc asked, ironically.

"I also heard Sheriff Johnny Behan was going to make you all stand trial for murder," Kyle added.

"He's a lapdog for the cowboys. Wyatt will testify for us."

"But you decided not to stay around for the trial?"

"Behan can issue a warrant for me," Doc said. "But he doesn't know I live here in Retribution. Unless someone tells him."

"None of my business," Kyle said.

"How'd you pick up Blackjack Shackleton's pocket watch?" Doc asked him.

"There's a ranch in Reeve Forest on the Kettleberg Road."

Doc nodded. "Sure. The Blaisdell place. Nice people. I had dinner with them in the spring."

"Blackjack and Taggart paid them a visit," Kyle said. "I found Blaisdell and both of his sons shot dead in the yard. I found his wife Sarah inside the house. She had been raped by Blackjack and left on the floor of her kitchen to die."

"You sure it was Shackleton?" Doc asked him.

"No doubt about it. I found this pocket watch held in Sarah Blaisdell's hand. It had been broken when Shackleton ripped it from her."

Kyle fished the ornate pocket watch from his vest coat pocket and showed it to Doc. He sprung the pocket watch open. It played *Greensleeves*. Kyle turned the pocket watch off.

"I found this lying beside her body. Blackjack probably doesn't realize it got torn off in the struggle or if he wouldn't have left it behind."

"Shackleton will know where it is now," Doc said.

"I'm counting on it," Kyle said. "That's why I showed it to Waco. He might pass the message on to Blackjack."

"Are you going after Shackleton and his outlaws?"

"I am aimin' to."

"I wish you good luck," Doc said.

Kyle stopped in front of the Crystal Palace Saloon. "Join me for a drink at the Crystal Palace?"

Doc shook his head. "Gunfighting has taken a toll on my painting. I have a sunset that I have to finish."

He walked down the boardwalk toward his cottage.

On the road that night, Hoss drove the Iron Maiden stage-coach through a violent storm. Beside him sat a marshal named Longfellow, on loan from Kettleberg, a rifle across his legs. Black clouds raced across the moon. Rain lashed the road. Thunder cracked as if it was rending the sky apart. Lightning exploded directly over the Iron Maiden. It struck a tree with a spectacular eruption of sparks in the darkness. Hoss pulled the Iron Maiden off the road, bypassing the fallen oak and managed to get the coach back up onto the road again. The iron panel behind Hoss opened and one of the guards, a deputy sheriff named Calvert, hauled himself up into the pouring rain. Calvert was short and stocky with a well-trimmed moustache and lively eyes.

"What happened?" he shouted to Hoss.

"Tree got split in half by lightning," Hoss shouted back. "Get back down inside! Do not open that hatch again even if we stop!"

Calvert nodded and closed the Iron Maiden's hatch. Hoss urged the horses on, then leaned forward, squinting through the downpour. He could barely see ten feet in front of him. It looked as if the road ahead was washed out. Hoss reined in the horses.

On a ridge above the bridge, Blackjack John Shackleton, Paul Taggart, Wendell Trask and three more gunmen from the wedding party waited on horseback. Way below them the Iron Maiden came to a stop at a washed-out bridge. Hoss jumped down and sloshed through the mud to the river's edge. Up on the coach, Marshal Longfellow looked out into the night. Behind him, the hatch was thrown back and Calvert crawled out.

Taggart put the long rifle to his shoulder and sighted through the modified spyglass. Through the magnified shot he could see Marshal Longfellow in the passenger seat up top. The spyglass travelled down to Calvert. Another Special Marshal named Spencer, in his twenties, climbed out of the Iron Maiden to see what was going on. Taggart lowered the spyglass.

Down at the washed-out bridge, Calvert jumped down and moved over to Hoss. Both of them had to shout above the noise of the storm.

"Do we turn back?" Calvert asked.

"No!" Hoss shouted back. "We'll take the Reeve Forest road to Retribution. Deke Reneker's got a safe at the Crystal Palace. Storm should blow over by morning."

They did not hear the sound of the gunshot over the cacophony of the storm. Marshal Spencer, sitting on top of the Iron Maiden, clutched his chest and fell down into the mud. Hoss and Calvert ran back to the Iron Maiden. Hoss grabbed his rifle. Calvert turned with his rifle aimed.

But at *what*?

Taggart fired down at the Iron Maiden.

Marshal Longfellow toppled from the top of the stagecoach. Deputy Calvert whirled, not knowing where the shots had come from, his eyes wild.

"Where the hell are they?" he shouted.

"In the trees!" Hoss shouted. "Back of that ridge!"

Hoss climbed up into the driver's seat of the Iron Maiden. Calvert climbed back into the iron hatch. Hoss grabbed the reins and turned the stagecoach away from the bridge.

Up on the hill, through the magnified sight of his rifle, Taggart had trouble seeing through the curtain of rain. It was so distorting that the Iron Maiden was only a shape moving against the downpour. Taggart lowered his high-powered rifle, shaking his head.

"I can't get another shot."

Wendell Trask said: "Hit one of the horses!"

Shackleton reached out to stop Taggart. "If that coach crashes down into the river we'll lose the gold in the torrent! There is only one place the driver can go on that road and that is back to Retribution."

"What happens then?" Trask asked.

"Deke Reneker will transfer the gold to his safe in the Crystal Palace Saloon for safe keeping," Shackleton said. "We'll hit it there."

The outlaws watched as the Iron Maiden kicked up the mud on the road far below them and was lost to sight.

On Saratoga Street the saloons were crowded, the boardwalks teeming with life. Waco was sitting on the porch of the Pacific Hotel. The rainstorm lashed the streets, driving people inside. Hoss drove the Iron Maiden down the street. Waco watched him turn down the side street beside the Crystal Palace Saloon.

Inside the Crystal Palace Saloon, Deke Reneker, Missy Vartan, Homer, Mayor Ballantyne, Swede and his wife were at a back table in an alcove. Missy Vartan had given another superb performance at the Music Hall Theater to an appreciative audience. The after-theater crowd in the saloon was boisterous and bawdy. Mayor Ballantyne was busy lighting a pipe which blew sweet-scented tobacco so thick Missy almost choked. Swede and his wife Hannah were gushing over Missy's stellar performance. Jim Plank moved over to Deke Reneker and whispered something urgently to him. Deke nodded and got to his feet.

"Excuse me for a moment," he said. "I am sure on this dark and stormy night our esteemed mayor can regale you all with a 'ghost' story."

Deke and Jim Plank moved away.

"I want to hear it!" Homer said enthusiastically. "Your stories are always real fanciful, Mr. Mayor!"

Missy Vartan suppressed a smile. Homer caught her eye and grinned. She thought she had established a strong bond with him when they had talked together in the deserted music hall.

"I am sure Homer and I would appreciate the opportunity to hear one of your stories, Mr. Mayor," she said.

Mayor Ballantyne leaned back, managing not to puff smoke right into Missy's face again. "A tempestuous night like this one does bring a recollection to my mind," the mayor began.

Deke emerged from the Crystal Palace Saloon into the pouring rain with Jim Plank. Hoss was waiting for them, mud-stained and disheveled, looking like some kind of a specter. Deputy Sheriff Calvert was with him. "Outlaws tried to hijack the gold shipment," Hoss said. "Two marshals are dead. The bridge at Falcon Point had washed out. I was headed for Denver to deliver the gold shipment. I need to store the gold in your safe for the night, Mr. Reneker. Then I can set out for Denver in the morning."

Deke took hold of the situation immediately. "Of course."

"I'll need help to get the Iron Maiden out of sight," Hoss said.

"The main street was deserted when we rode in," Calvert said.

"Jim will help you," Deke said, turning to Plank. "When you are done, drive the Iron Maiden into the livery. I will talk to Moses. He will be waiting for you."

Plank accompanied Hoss and Calvert down the street.

Clancy's Steakhouse was on a corner diagonally across from the side street outside the Crystal Palace Saloon. Kyle was in there eating a steak. He was the only one in the restaurant on a filthy night like this. He watched Hoss Cavanaugh, Deputy Sheriff Calvert and Jim Plank carry the heavy bags from the Iron Maiden up the narrow wooden steps along the side of the building that led to Deke's second-floor balcony.

From the front room in her house, Rachel watched some riders silhouetted in the downpour. She thought it might be Blackjack Shackleton and the other outlaws returning, but they were too far away for her to be sure. They were just ghostly shapes in the torrent of rain.

A face suddenly leered at her in reflection. Rachel gasped, leaping to her feet. She whirled around to face Sheriff Tom Shaw. He was wild-eyed, clutching at Rachel. He was also looking out the window.

"Outlaws," he murmured, deliriously.

Rachel steadied him. "Just riders in the storm. I do not know who they are. They don't appear to be heading here."

"I have to stop them."

"You are not going anywhere, Tom, except back to bed. You are burning up with fever." She moved him back to the bedroom with her. "You've got to lie down, Sheriff. Those stitches are going to have to hold up and you are weak as a kitten."

"I killed three of them!" Shaw murmured. "They will want revenge. Take it out on innocent people."

"You will stop them," Rachel said. "But not tonight."

In the bedroom Rachel laid Sheriff Shaw back down on the bed and covered him with a blanket. He was trembling. Immediately his eyes closed. Rachel looked at him with compassion in her eyes.

Another storm had descended onto Retribution. Thunder forked over the clouds, bringing with it a new onslaught of rain. People were hurrying from the streets to get into the restaurants and the saloons along the boardwalk.

Outside the telegraph office, Shackleton and the others dismounted. Waco stepped out of the shadows. Across the street they could see the glowing lights of the Crystal Palace Saloon and hear the faint piano music drifting from inside.

Waco nodded at the saloon. "The gold shipment has been transferred to Deke Reneker's safe upstairs," he said. "The only law in town is Deputy Larchmont and he is running scared. I tangled with Kyle Bascomb, but he ain't wearing a Marshal's badge. It won't be his fight."

Paul Taggart shook his head. "I thought I'd left that son of a bitch for dead on the road outside Retribution."

"He had a bullet crease across his forehead," Waco said. "I guess your aim ain't what it used to be, Taggart." He turned back to Shackleton and his voice was softer. "He's carrying your pocket watch."

Shackleton stared at Waco in shock. He felt in his pockets, only now realizing that the pocket watch had gone, his vest torn. He and Taggart exchanged a glance, realizing where Shackleton had lost it and where Kyle must have picked it up.

"He must have visited the Blaisdell place," Shackleton said. "Only place he could have found it."

"I know that watch has some sentimental value for you," Waco said.

"It surely does. We will pay Kyle Bascomb a visit. But first we need to pay our respects to Deke Reneker."

Inside the livery stable, Hoss had unhitched the team of horses from the coach with Deputy Sheriff Calvert and tied them up. A powerful, handsome black man, Moses waved aside the money Hoss tried to hand him.

"Mr. Reneker done taken care of this," he told them.

"Feed and water the horses, Moses," Hoss said. "I am leaving town at first light."

"Sure thing, Hoss."

Inside Clancy's Steakhouse, Kyle had just ordered more coffee. Rain continued to drench the town as Trask moved down a side street toward the back of the Crystal Palace Saloon. Blackjack Shackleton, Waco and the other two outlaws moved to the front doors of the saloon. Wendell Taggart climbed the stairs to Deke's balcony and opened a door that led to a corridor outside Deke's room. Kyle had not seen where Taggart and Trask and the other outlaws had gone, but there was no mistaking Shackleton's intent. Kyle had to remind himself that he was *not* the law in Retribution. But he still carried a Marshal's badge under his coat. Whatever Blackjack Shackleton and his outlaws were planning, they were not his concern.

But Kyle drank his coffee with an uneasy feeling in the pit of his stomach.

Shackleton, Waco and the two outlaws entered the Crystal Palace Saloon. The piano stopped playing. Conversations lowered to a minimum. There was a stunned silence. Shackleton pulled his gun, but he did not aim it at anyone.

"Saloon's closed for the night, folks," he said, affably. "Everybody out."

People begin to clear out fast. Behind the bar, the relief bartender went for the shotgun he had stashed there. Waco threw his Bowie knife and buried it in the man's chest. He collapsed. At a signal from Deke Reneker, Billy took his place at the bar. Missy Vartan took hold of Homer's hand. Mayor Ballantyne had paused in the middle of one of his tall stories. More people ran out of the saloon. Deke was on his feet now, facing Shackleton.

"What do you want, Blackjack?" Deke asked him.

On the second floor landing, Taggart appeared, his gun drawn.

Shackleton looked over at Deke Reneker, his tone relaxed. "The gold in your safe."

The saloon was almost empty now. A couple of men in seersucker suits, in their forties, stood nervously. One of them was named Holdeker. He said: "We're here from Fort Laramie. Thinking about opening a bank in Retribution. We just got in a few hours ago. We do not belong here."

"Sit down and enjoy your whiskey," Shackleton said.

Trask entered from the back with the other outlaws. He stopped the last three saloon girls from leaving. He smiled lasciviously. "Stay with us for a spell. It might be a long night."

The saloon girls kept together. Deke Reneker faced Shackleton. "Let my son and Miss Vartan go."

Mayor Ballantyne jumped up. "Yes, of course, I'll be happy to take the lad outside and escort Miss Vartan back to her hotel."

"They stay and you stay, Mr. Mayor," Shackleton said. "Swede, you and your wife can go. Piano player can stay."

Reluctantly Swede gripped his wife's hand and they hustled out of the saloon. Shackleton smiled at Deke. "We'll wait out the storm together, shall we?"

At that moment Hoss entered the Crystal Palace Saloon through the front doors. He took in the situation in an instant and slammed his rifle barrel against Shackleton's head. He went down hard. Hoss had not seen Taggart standing on the second floor landing. He fired at Hoss. The rifle dropped from Hoss's hands, blood seeping down one arm.

Trask rushed down the staircase and helped Shackleton onto a chair. His stomach wound had opened up again.

"Get the Doc," Shackleton said. "You know where to find her?"

"Yeah," Waco said. "I'll bring her here."

He moved out of the Crystal Palace Saloon. Three cowboys had been about to enter.

"Saloon's closed for the night, boys," Waco said.

Something in the way he said it made them back off and head for the Last Chance Saloon on the next corner. Two of Shackleton's men took their place at the front door to discourage further customers.

Waco climbed onto his horse and rode toward Dr. Drake's house.

Inside Doc's cottage, Doc was painting on a new canvas. A scuff of sound caught his attention. He glanced up. "I had better start locking that back gate," he said mildly.

Skeeter had let herself in through the gate and latched it behind her. She moved forward tentatively to where Doc was painting another sunset.

"You sure got the eye for color, Doc. What are you going to call this one?"

"It doesn't have a name yet."

"It is sure pretty, whatever you're gonna call it. I do not rightly know how you get those brush strokes so even-like. You must have a picture in your mind of the painting even before you start on it. Like all of the images are all there in your head just waitin' to be born."

"You have a colorful way with words, Skeeter," Doc said. "But that is not what you came to see me about."

"No, it ain't. I been trying to find the right words." She moved right up to him. Her voice was clear, but soft. "I was there, Doc. I was in Tombstone."

Doc nodded. "Yes, I saw you." He set down his paintbrush. He grabbed Skeeter by her arms and held her tightly. "Why did you follow me?"

For a moment Skeeter squirmed in his grasp, then she gave up, her voice plaintive. "I didn't know you were heading to Tombstone. When I followed you there, I had a bad feelin' about what was going to happen. You said you were friends with Wyatt Earp. I recognized him right away. He was standing with you and his brothers. I could not hear what you were all sayin', but I knew that it was important. I could sense it with every part of my being. When you and the Earp brothers walked down Fremont Street, I knew in my heart there was goin' be a shootout. I followed you to the OK Corral. I did not think you had seen me."

"I saw you," Doc said, brusquely. "You could've been hit by a stray bullet! Your dad is lying gut-shot at Dr. Drake's place and your mom needs you, Skeeter. I am no one for you to be pining over."

"I can't help it, Doc," Skeeter said. "I wouldn't want something bad to happen to you."

Doc let her go and turned his attention back to his painting. "I allow you have feelings for me, Skeeter, misguided as they may be. Anyway, it has come to my attention that you are leaving Retribution."

"Not until my dad recovers from his injuries. He will be laid up for quite a spell, the way I see it. My mom is getting everything packed up for us to leave town, but I reckon that will not happen anytime soon. She is a dreamer. Besides, she needs to open up the school again. So I am going to be here with you until you kick me out like I was a mangy dog in the street."

Doc smiled in spite of himself. "You have been getting under my feet for a spell."

"But we're friends, ain't we?"

"I will give it some thought."

"This is all I can ask of you."

"I am not your concern, Skeeter. Are we clear on that?"

"Yes, sir," Skeeter said, emphatically nodding her head. "I am real sorry. It will not happen again." Then she grinned. "But, shit, Doc! That gunfight in Tombstone was sure excitin."

"Language, Skeeter."

"Sorry."

"I have some painting to do," Doc said. "You are interrupting my concentration."

"But are we still friends?"

"I might consider counting you among them. That would make two," he added, sardonically.

"You and Wyatt Earp," Skeeter said.

"That would be about right."

"How about Marshal Bascomb?" Skeeter asked him.

"I'll allow for three," Doc said.

The gate swung open and Kyle entered the back patio. He looked at Skeeter, then back at Doc. "Seems like Abigail is here more often than anyone else."

"She was just leaving," Doc said. He took a look at Kyle's face. "What has happened?"

"Blackjack Shackleton and his men have taken prisoners at the Crystal Palace Saloon," Kyle said. "That singer

Missy Vartan, the mayor, Deke Reneker, a couple of dudes I did not know and the saloon girls. I reckon there was about eight hostages in all."

Now Skeeter was frightened. "Homer too?"

Kyle nodded. "He's in the saloon as well."

Doc turned back to his painting and put a few brush strokes on it. His voice was ironic. "Any reason you're sharing this fascinating but irrelevant piece of information with me, Marshal?"

Kyle shrugged. "I could use some back-up," he said, quietly.

11

Crystal Palace

DOC ALLOWED THAT to percolate, then he turned back to his painting. "I do not want to get into the habit of helping lawmen. Might be harmful to my health."

"I'm resigning as a marshal on Sunday," Kyle said.

"Always good news for me."

Skeeter ran to Doc, the words tumbling out. "Please, Doc! Homer's my best friend! Next to you, of course. That ruffian rat ain't got a whit of brains, he'll try an' be a hero cause he's brave and stupid. Please go with the marshal."

"I got a score to settle with Blackjack Shackleton," Kyle said, "but that don't mean you have. Just wanted to know if you wanted to throw your hand with me this one time. Your call."

Doc stopped painting and stared at the sunset that was taking shape on the easel. Suddenly he got up and walked into the front room. He came back with a holster wrapped in cashmere. Skeeter's eyes shone as she watched Doc unwrap his pearl-handled gun and strapped it on. He took hold of her shoulders.

"You go home now," he said. "Stay with your mother. I will bring Homer over to see you when this is done. You promise me?"

"I do, Doc!"

Skeeter turned and vanished out the back. The gate slammed. Kyle shook his head.

"Doc Holliday has a heart. Never thought I would see the day."

"You won't if you repeat that to anyone," Doc said. "Who are we going up against?"

"Blackjack Shackleton, Paul Taggart and Wendell Trask."

"Is there a back entrance?"

"Staircase behind the saloon. Leads up to the rooms on the second floor."

"Locked?"

"I guess we'll find that out," Kyle said.

"If Homer is in that saloon, Skeeter will find a way to be with him," Doc said. "She would not leave him on his own. Who are the other hostages?"

"Mayor Ballantyne."

"Hardly counts."

"That songbird who came in on the stage yesterday," Kyle said. "Missy Vartan. She has a history with Deke Reneker. Shackleton let Swede and his wife go, but he hung onto a couple of fellahs who were in town from Fort Laramie. Billy is tending bar. He is a hothead. but I reckon he will not make a play for Blackjack unless the notion takes him to be a hero."

"Is Tom Shaw still out at Rachel's place?" Doc asked.

"He is. He might not make it. Which leaves us with no law in Retribution."

"You still carrying your Marshal's badge?" Doc asked him.

"I was going to hand it in to the Territorial Marshal in St. Louis, but I reckon I'll wait awhile. I did deputize you in Tombstone, but that was a personal fight."

Doc looked at Kyle, as if ironic. "And this isn't?"

"I got a score to settle with Blackjack Shackleton. That don't make this your fight."

"Skeeter is my responsibility."

Kyle was also ironic. "So you have adopted her?"

Doc shrugged. "Seems to be that way."

"Are we together in this?"

"We are."

Waco rode up to Dr. Drake's house and dismounted. He tied up his horse and pushed through the front door. Rachel had seen him ride up.

"You're needed at the Crystal Palace, Doctor," Waco said. "It is Blackjack Shackleton. His stitches tore loose."

"I will get my bag," Rachel said, immediately.

Waco looked over the front of the house. "Where is your patient?"

"He died about an hour ago," Rachel said. "The undertaker was just here."

"Is that a fact? Maybe I will take a look around just to make sure."

Before Rachel could stop him, Waco walked through the front room of the house and threw open the bedroom door.

The bedroom was deserted.

The bed had been smoothed out. Rachel followed him, but her unease was apparent. Waco moved to a closet and threw it open. It was full of clothes. He shut the closet and gave the bedroom a cursory glance.

"You going to search the whole house?" Rachel asked, pointedly. "If Blackjack Shackleton has taken a turn for the worst, I need to get to Retribution."

Waco nodded. "You do, Doc."

He moved out of the bedroom. Rachel closed the bedroom door. She knew there was only one place where Sheriff Tom Shaw could have hidden himself. That was behind the bedroom door where there was just enough room for him to have hunkered down. He waited until he heard Rachel and Waco leaving the house and the front door slammed. He had to grasp a bookcase in the corner to steady himself. He was bathed in sweat. He heard the sound of Waco and Rachel riding away from the house. Shaw picked up his gun belt where he had hidden it under the covers and strapped it on with trembling hands.

In Doc Holiday's cottage in Retribution, Doc was suddenly racked with a coughing fit. Kyle waited until it had passed. "You need to see Dr. Drake."

"No need," Doc said. "A cough like this doesn't go away."

Kyle nodded. "I will allow for that," he said.

He and Doc moved through the patio door out into the street. They walked down the boardwalk in the driving rain. They split up. Doc headed for the wooden staircase leading up to the second floor of the Crystal Palace Saloon. Kyle crossed the street, then paused when he saw Waco and Rachel ride up. They dismounted, Rachel carrying her distinctive doctor's black bag. They moved inside the saloon. Kyle jumped up onto the boardwalk, but he did not approach the saloon where Shackleton had posted guards outside.

Inside the Crystal Palace Saloon, the piano player was playing under duress. Deke Reneker, Missy Vartan and Mayor Ballantyne sat together at their table. The two bankers sat at another table, motionless. The saloon girls were undaunted, but they sat together at one table. Billy was tending bar. Waco motioned Rachel to tend to Blackjack Shackleton, but she stopped beside Hoss Cavanaugh.

"How bad is it?" she asked him, setting her doctor's bag down and opening it.

"I think my arm is broken," Hoss muttered.

Rachel nodded. "Yes, it is, in two places. I will have to put it into a makeshift splint and then into a sling."

Waco moved over to Rachel and dragged her to her feet. "Blackjack is the one you're here to tend."

Rachel stood her ground, then she turned to Deke Reneker. "You can tend to Hoss. Bind his arm tight and make a sling."

Billy looked at Deke, who nodded. "Do like the doctor said."

Billy came around the bar with a knotted kerchief for the sling and some bandages. Only then did Rachel move to where Blackjack Shackleton sat in a hardbacked chair, clearly in pain. Rachel unbuttoned his shirt and noted where the bandage had come apart. Blood seeped out from under it.

"You have lost a lot of blood," Rachel told him, reaching into her doctor's bag. "I will bind the wound, but I would recommend you go to the hospital in Philadelphia."

"I will be just fine right here," Shackleton told her, his teeth gritted against the pain.

Waco knelt beside the fallen bartender and pulled his Bowie knife out of his chest, wiping it clean. When she looked at him, Rachel noted the fallen shotgun lying beside the slain bartender's body.

At the side of the Crystal Palace Saloon, Doc climbed the stairs to Deke's balcony. Something caught his eye. He looked down the wooden staircase and saw Skeeter pulling back two slats of wood under the stairs. Obviously, she had a secret way into the saloon that only she and Homer knew about. She disappeared into the Crystal Palace Saloon. Doc tried the door on the second-floor balcony, found it open and moved inside.

Inside the Crystal Palace Saloon, Skeeter snuck down a back part of the saloon to where it opened up into the main room. She crouched down, hidden by a table. She noted the players inside the saloon. Billy, the main bartender, was tending to Hoss Cavanaugh who had been shot. He did not seem to be badly hurt. The other bartender who had worked at the Crystal Palace Saloon lay dead. Skeeter looked over and noted Waco in the saloon with his Bowie knife sheathed in his belt. She had seen Waco once before in Retribution and she knew he had dealings with Blackjack Shackleton. That singer Missy Vartan was sitting at one of the saloon tables. Beside her was Mayor Ballantyne. For once he was not pontificating on the foibles of the human spirit. His great toad face was passive and pinched. A couple of businessmen whom Skeeter had not seen before were at one of the other tables. They looked like city slickers who just happened to find themselves in the wrong place at the wrong time. They were talking together, their conversation muted and subdued. At the head of the first table was Deke Reneker. Skeeter had always got along with Deke, even though her father had told her once that he was not a person to be trusted. As if Sheriff Tom Shaw could make that distinction, Skeeter thought. But she had always liked Deke Reneker because he did not treat her like a snot-nose little brat. She looked over at the last person in the saloon and her heart thudded in her chest. It was *Homer*! She reckoned he had snuck into the saloon the same way that she had. He knew the secret way to get into the saloon. In fact, he knew the way to skulk into *all* of the saloons! Skeeter prayed that for once the ruffian-rat kept his mouth shut and did not cause any trouble. She scooted back into the shadows at the side of the bar to watch.

Rachel was kneeling beside Blackjack Shackleton and redressed his wound. Shackleton had turned to the bankers who were watching him with fearful eyes.

"You'll find out that Mr. Reneker here runs this town of Retribution, gentlemen," he said. "Got people's hopes and dreams right in his pocket. He decides who prospers and who fails."

Deke had tight hold of Missy Vartan's hand. "I don't put a gun to people's heads," he said.

"You don't need to," Shackleton said. "You'd cut your own son's throat if you thought it would benefit you financially."

Homer leapt to his feet. "That's not true! You take that back!"

"Be quiet, Homer!" Skeeter said under her breath. "You ain't got the sense of a wood mouse!"

Outside of the Crystal Palace Saloon, the two outlaws guarding the front entrance spread out as Kyle strolled to within fifteen feet of them. Otis Larchmont walked up from the sheriff's office, bending under the weight of the deluge. He was carrying a shotgun The outlaws moved even farther apart as Otis faced them.

"Throw down your guns," he shouted.

They drew on the deputy marshal and fired. Otis dropped the first one, but he took a bullet, falling head-first into the mud. Kyle pulled his gun and fired, killing the second outlaw. He knelt beside Otis, who waved him on.

"I am all right," he said through gritted teeth. "Take care of things in the saloon."

Kyle straightened, looking down in the torrent of rain. No one else was on the street. Kyle moved toward the doors of the saloon.

Doc Holliday entered Deke Reneker's office to find the safe there was open. Jim Plank was transferring bags of gold into saddlebags that were open on Deke's desk. He spun around and went for his gun. Doc pistol-whipped him and he crashed to the floor, out cold.

Up on the second-floor balcony of the Crystal Palace Saloon, Wendell Trask ran toward Deke's apartment, swinging up his rifle.

Kyle came through the swing doors of the saloon, firing his revolver. He dropped one of Shackleton's men. Paul Taggart fired on him from the back of the saloon, Waco in the front. Kyle dove to the floor, firing back. Shackleton hurled Rachel to one side and drew on Kyle, who was a helpless target on the floor.

Deke Reneker slipped a small derringer into his hand from under the table and fired, hitting Shackleton.

Homer spotted Skeeter under one of the tables and ran toward her.

Skeeter jumped up from her hiding place, shouting at him. "Homer, stay put!"

Waco turned and fired at Homer.

Deke Reneker jumped in front of his son, knocking him to one side, taking the bullet in the chest. He threw his body over Homer to protect him.

Hoss pushed the three saloon girls back out of the line of fire.

Kyle came up onto one knee and fired, hitting Waco in the shoulder.

On the second floor landing Wendell Trask fired on Doc. He ducked down, firing his pearl-handed .45 revolver. He hit Trask and sent him back into the railing. It split apart and Trask fell to the saloon floor.

The last two of Shackleton's men in the saloon fired their weapons. Kyle fanned his gun, blowing the gunmen away.

Mayor Ballantyne cringed back, cowering behind an overturned table.

Homer crawled out from under his father's body. Missy Vartan kneeled and lifted Deke up into her arms. His eyes focused on her. His voice was barely audible.

"Homer…"

"He is all right," Missy said, distraught.

"Take care of him…"

Missy Vartan cradled Deke in her arms. "No talking. Save your strength. The doctor is right here."

Deke smiled up at her. "For once I did the right thing."

Missy looked at him through her tears. "You did," she said.

"Always a first time," Deke said, with irony.

Homer knelt down beside his father. Skeeter knelt down with him. Deke turned his head to the boy.

"Be mindful of your ma…"

At first Homer did not understand. Then he looked at Missy Vartan and the realization of what he had just heard sank into him.

Missy Vartan was his mother.

Tears flooded Homer's eyes. Skeeter grabbed his hand and held it tightly in both of her own.

Deke Reneker fell back into Missy's arms as death claimed him.

Trask staggered to his feet in front of the bar. He pulled his gun and aimed it at Kyle's back.

Rachel grabbed the fallen shotgun. "For Samuel," she said, breathlessly.

She fired both barrels. Trask was blown back into the mirror beside the piano. It shattered as he slid to the floor, dead.

Outside in the Retribution street, Sheriff Tom Shaw dismounted and tied his horse to the hitching post. He was still in a lot of pain, but he knew what he had to do.

12

Aftermath

PAUL TAGGART GRABBED Missy Vartan, dragging her away from Deke's body. Waco put a gun to her head, the hammer cocked back. Doc was coming down the sweeping staircase from the second floor. Kyle whirled around.

"Anyone shoots," Taggart shouted out, "she dies."

Taggart and Waco moved fast through the saloon with Missy Vartan as their hostage. Shackleton, badly wounded, went with them. They burst out through the side saloon doors.

Sheriff Tom Shaw moved through the storm toward the Crystal Palace Saloon. He was unsteady on his feet, but thinking fast. Blackjack Shackleton mounted his horse with difficulty. Taggart climbed onto his horse. Waco hoisted Missy Vartan up onto his mount, then pulled himself up after her. Waco's .45 revolver stayed positioned at her head. Behind them in the street, Otis Larchmont climbed to his feet, but he was too late. Shackleton, Taggart and Waco galloped down Saratoga Street.

Sheriff Tom Shaw aimed at Waco and fired. The bullet grazed Waco's arm, the gun barrel jerking away from

Missy's head. She leapt off the horse, falling heavily to the churning ground. Tom Shaw fired at Blackjack but missed him. Shackleton took aim at the sheriff and fired. Tom Shaw crumpled to the ground. Shackleton, Taggart and Waco rode on, their horses' hooves splashing mud across Shaw's inert figure.

Kyle ran out of the Crystal Palace Saloon. He mounted his horse and went after the three outlaws. Otis Larchmont and Rachel picked up Missy Vartan from the street. Skeeter ran out of the saloon over to where her father was lying on the ground. Doc Holliday was beside her. Gently he turned the sheriff over.

Tom Shaw was dead.

Skeeter collapsed into Doc's arms, sobbing uncontrollably. Doc put his arms around the girl and held her close.

On the road outside Retribution, Kyle pulled up on his horse. Blackjack Shackleton, Paul Taggart and Waco had disappeared into the ravages of the storm. Kyle slid his rifle back into its scabbard and turned back to Retribution.

Three days later the storm has blown itself out. A stagecoach stood outside the livery stable. Old Moses had finished hitching up the team. Hoss was back in Retribution. He had delivered his gold shipment to Denver in good time. His arm was still in a sling. He cinched down the last of the luggage on top of the stagecoach. Rooster, a gangling assistant, was helping him.

Missy Vartan stood in Deke Reneker's apartment on the second floor of the Crystal Palace Saloon. It was nicely furnished with antiques and Chinese screens everywhere. She looked around the sumptuous room seeing little touches of Deke Reneker everywhere. She had delayed her departure from Retribution, but now it was time for her to leave. Idly, she moved over to a Cherry wood desk, not sure what she was looking for, opening the little drawers. She found a gold locket nestled in cloth and unwrapped it. Behind her she did not even hear Jim Plank enter the room. Missy opened the locket. There were two photographs inside. One showed Deke Reneker as a young man, barely out of his teen years. The other picture was of Missy Vartan, looking radiant, also young, her hair curled about her head in brunette ringlets.

Jim Plank cleared his throat, as not to intrude on her reverie. "The boss looked at that locket a good deal. He said it was his lucky charm."

Missy Vartan turned to him, surprised. "Did he say that?"

"Yes, ma'am. I didn't mean to startle you none."

"You did not. I just wanted something to remember Deke by. We shared a lot of memories here in Retribution. It seems a cruel trick of fate that he is gone."

"Yes, ma'am. I am sure the boss would have wanted you to have that locket. I was just coming to tell you the stage was ready for passengers. But you can take your time. Hoss Cavanaugh never left Retribution on time in his life."

"You worked for Mr. Reneker for a long time, didn't you?" Missy said. "What was your name again?"

"Jim Plank, ma'am. Yes, I worked for Mr. Reneker for over twenty years."

"People in the town did not trust him. He could be ruthless and callous, but there was a caring side to him also. You could see that in the way he doted on his son. Not many people in town even knew that Homer was his child."

"But *you* did?" Plank asked her.

There was a long pause while Missy looked around the room, as if she were saying goodbye. "Did you that know that Homer was my son with Deke?"

That revelation rocked Jim Plank. He stared at her. Missy sighed. "I don't know if it was much of a secret. Homer looked so much like Deke." She turned back to Plank. "May I have this locket as a memento?"

Plank found his voice. "Mr. Reneker would want you to have it."

"That's very kind." Missy curled the locket and put it in a sequined bag. "Your boss could be a deceitful, violent man. I have no illusions about that. I am sure there were times when you helped him carry out various nefarious deeds. I know that, too. But that did not stop me from loving him."

"Yes, ma'am."

"Will you escort me to the stage, Mr. Plank?"

"It would be my honor ma'am," Jim Plank said.

Missy Vartan looked once more at the suite of rooms, then followed Jim Plank to the corridor leading down into the Crystal Palace Saloon.

Outside on the Retribution street, Hoss Cavanaugh helped Missy Vartan's three musicians into the stagecoach. Alice Shaw stood beside the coach.. Homer stood nearby, in his best Sunday clothes, looking for Skeeter. Mayor Ballantyne was waxing poetic about something fittingly obscure. Half the town had come to see the two families off.

Doc Holliday and Skeeter walked down the boardwalk. She was dressed in a gingham dress with high-buttoned shoes, looking for all the world as if she were already a young woman. She was trying to keep a tight rein on her emotions.

"Once my father died, there was no call for ma to stay here," Skeeter said. "Too many memories." She looked around the main street. "I am not going to miss Retribution," she proclaimed. "Not the tiniest little bit. Godforsaken, stinking mudhole. Philadelphia is a *real* city with wide streets and beautiful buildings where people do not kill each other over a poker hand. There is history there."

"There is," Doc said.

"I am going to be a history teacher," she proclaimed.

"A noble ambition for a young woman to aspire to," he allowed.

"Even for a ragamuffin brat like me?"

"Especially in that case."

"You won't forget me, will ya, Doc? Promise me you will always keep a kind thought about me in your heart." Skeeter could not go on. Her lower lip quivered. "I am gonna miss you, Doc."

"You will be traveling all the way east with your best friend."

"I lied about Homer being my best friend." Skeeter said. "*You* are."

Skeeter turned into Doc Holliday's arms. He held her close. He started to cough and muffled it with his handkerchief.

"You take care of your mother," Doc said. "Alice Shaw is a fine lady. And take care of Homer."

"I *am* going to be a teacher," Skeeter told him through her tears.

"Being a teacher, imparting knowledge, that would make me proud of you. Time for you to go, Skeeter."

"I am prepared," she said, stiffly.

Skeeter broke from him, sniffling back her tears. Doc's coughing fit had passed, but Skeeter noted the little drops of blood on his handkerchief.

"Don't you go back to gunslinging and get yourself shot," she said. "Take something for that cough. Finish that sunset painting of Retribution for me."

"I will give it some thought," Doc said.

"Goodbye, Doc."

"Goodbye, Skeeter."

Impulsively Skeeter kissed him on the cheek, then ran to the stagecoach. Hoss had jumped down and was helping Alice Shaw inside. Skeeter looked for Homer and waved at him impatiently.

"Come on, ya ruffian rat! What are you waiting for? Get in here!"

Homer broke into a sprint for the stagecoach. Kyle stepped up beside Doc Holliday.

"When did Hoss get back from delivering his gold?" he asked.

"Last night," Doc said. "I kept thinking maybe I should have helped myself to just one bag."

Kyle smiled. "That thought crossed my mind too. Why didn't you?"

"Might've weighed on my conscience."

Kyle shot him a wry look. "And mine."

Missy Vartan was talking quietly with Otis Larchmont, his arm in a sling, who now wore a Sheriff's badge on his coat lapel. Doc followed Kyle's gaze.

"So Missy Vartan is Homer's mother?" Doc asked.

"I don't believe it was much of a secret," Kyle said. "But Homer did not know until last night. Swede is going to run the Crystal Palace Saloon."

"That makes sense," Doc said. "Are you heading out after Blackjack Shackleton?"

"I aim to," Kyle said. "But I don't hold out much hope of finding him or Paul Taggart."

"You comin' back to Retribution for Rachel?" Doc asked.

Kyle shook his head. "It's better for her if I don't."

"I will allow that might be true," Doc said. "Does she know that?"

"She does. It is better for her this way."

"But not for you," Doc said.

"Probably not," Kyle allowed.

At the stagecoach, Skeeter grabbed Homer's hand when he reached her. She pushed him into the stagecoach and climbed up after him. Kyle looked at her.

"You will miss Skeeter," he said to Doc.

Doc shook his head. "She's a kid. She will forget. I am sure I will never see her again. Do not bother to drop by my place. I am out of the helping the marshal business."

Doc started to cough rackingly again and walked away. Kyle called out after him.

"Doc…"

Doc waved a dismissive hand at him, nodding. "I know. Fix that cough, take in the vapors, do not gamble, try not to kill anyone. Sure is a laundry list you've got there, Marshal."

Doc turned the corner where his house was located and disappeared. Missy Vartan climbed into the stagecoach. Mayor Ballantyne bowed obsequiously. Hoss climbed to the top and stirred up the horses. The stagecoach took off down Saratoga Street out of Retribution.

Ten years later...

Doc Holliday went into Kettleberg every three months for supplies. As always, he was immaculately dressed in a black frock coat and black boots with a black string bowtie at his throat. He wore a velvet waistcoat with a gold watch chain on it. He would stock up on cheeses, butter, eggs, sausages, huckleberry biscuits, spiced beef, potatoes, Virginia ham, pork and beans and Folger's pre-roasted coffee. Most of his provisions he bought from Swede's Mercantile and Grocery Store. Swede and his wife had finally packed their general store and moved to Kettleberg where Swede did a flourishing business. The townspeople flocked to it and Doc was glad to see that Swede had found a home to replace Retribution. Swede was always happy to see Doc Holliday, but his visits were of concern to Swede and his wife, who now worked in the store.

"That cough of yours is getting worse," Swede said. "I said the very same to Mama the last time you came in."

Swede's wife, Hannah, was putting together Doc's order. "Ja, that is right. You do not take care of yourself, Doc. I have a home remedy from the Old Country which will cure colic, cramps in the stomach and cholera. I will mix up a potion for you when you return from the saloon."

Doc nodded. This was a continuing conversation he endured to appease them. "That is most kind of you, Mrs. Norquist. I will surely make myself available to whatever remedy you recommend."

Hannah was very pleased and went about loading up Doc's supplies. Swede looked at Doc with sorrowful eyes. "One of these days you will come into our store and expire right here on the floor."

"Hush, Swede, that is quite enough," Hannah scolded him.

Doc left them with the order and made his way to the Lucky Dollar Saloon on Truscott Street in Kettleberg. There was always a poker game in a back room of the establishment which Doc periodically sat in on. He was careful not be seen winning too much because, as far as Doc knew, no one in Kettleberg knew who he was. He answered to 'Doc', but his fellow poker players had no idea of his reputation as a gambler, never mind as a gunfighter. Which suited Doc just fine.

During the last few years, Doc had taken to strolling down to the river in Kettleberg with a beautiful doctor whom Kyle Bascomb had once known in Retribution. Her name was Dr. Rachel Drake and she had a thriving practice in the town. Doc never brought up Kyle's name, as it had been many years since he had seen him.

"There is no cure for that cough of yours unless you get treatment," Rachel told him.

"A marshal of my acquaintance once spent many years trying to remedy that situation," Doc allowed. "He never succeeded either."

Rachel stopped beside the fast-flowing river, looking at Doc's face. "Does your marshal have a name?"

It was a question Doc had been expecting for many years. "Kyle Bascomb," he told her.

The news stunned Rachel. She continued to stroll down the river with Doc, trying to compose herself. "I knew him," she finally said.

"Figured as much."

"You have never mentioned him on our walks together."

"I did not want to bring up a delicate matter," Doc said. "None of my business."

"But the two of you were very close friends," Rachel objected.

"Kyle was a U.S. Federal Marshal. As far as he was concerned, I was a notorious gunfighter and our paths happened to converge on occasion for a time. Do not go reading anything more into it than that."

"There was a lot more to it than that!" Rachel insisted. "You know there was!"

"It was a lot of years ago," Doc said. "Best forget about it now."

Rachel nodded. She and Doc walked along the riverbank in silence. Then she said: "Kyle Bascomb handed me an ultimatum. Leave Retribution with him or he would move on. I had to decline his offer. It would have destroyed both of us. He left Retribution the next day. I never saw him again."

"So you pulled up stakes and came here to Kettleberg," Doc said.

"I got offered a place as a physician here. I took it. It was the best choice I could have made. I love my life here. My patients are wonderful. The old doctor retired soon after I took over his practice." She looked at Doc shrewdly. "But you already knew all of this."

"Some part of it," Doc allowed. "But meeting up with you after all of these years has been a kindness."

Rachel looked away at the fast-flowing river. It was the question she had steeled herself to ask. "Do you want know what happened to Marshal Kyle Bascomb?"

"I do not," Doc said. "I know he handed in his Marshal's badge to the marshal in St. Louis."

"What happened to the town of Retribution?"

"An epidemic of cholera broke out that ravaged most of the townspeople."

"But not Kyle?" Rachel asked, quickly.

"No, he had left by that time," Doc said. "I never heard from him after that."

"What became of the town?" Rachel asked.

"It died," Doc said, simply.

Rachel stopped walking and turned to him. "But I remember you told Swede and his wife Hannah that *you* were still living in Retribution."

Doc nodded. His eyes never left her face. "I am."

"But how can that be?"

Doc shrugged. "It's a ghost town now," he said.

13

Ghost Town

THAT STOPPED RACHEL in her tracks. "You can't be serious?"

Doc smiled. "I am the only living person residing in the town of Retribution. Once the cholera epidemic had passed, more and more folks just moved away. In the end I was the only one left."

"But you can't live in a town that has been abandoned!" Rachel exclaimed.

"It is my home. I come into Kettleberg every few weeks for supplies. Make sure Swede and his wife are doing well. And I look forward to the pleasure of your company on some days. Suits me just fine."

Rachel took Doc's arm as they strolled further along the river. She was obviously troubled by Doc's revelation about Kyle Bascomb. "But you don't know where Kyle travelled to after he turned in his Marshal's badge and left St. Louis?"

"I do not."

"I guess the past should be buried," she said, softly.

"If it does not, it will come back to haunt you," Doc said.

Rachel nodded. She knew that was true.

Sometime after that, Doc said goodbye to Swede and Hannah and loaded up his buckboard with the supplies he had purchased in Kettleberg. Clouds had rolled above him. Another storm was threatening. Doc urged the horses down Truscott Street, heading out into the country en route to Retribution.

A rider mounted his horse outside the Lucky Dollar Saloon in the town and followed Doc at a good distance.

The year was 1892.

By the time Doc Holliday reached Retribution the storm had hit with a vengeance. Thunder rolled and cracked. Lightning exploded out of the darkness. Doc pulled the buckboard under the shelter of some overhanging oak tree branches. There were no lights in his house. Or, for that matter, in any of the dilapidated buildings or the store fronts along Retribution's Saratoga Street. One of the broken shutters outside the Longhorn Dining Room in the Pacific Hotel banged in the gusting wind.

Doc unlocked his front door and brought the provisions through the living room into his modest kitchen area. He unbuckled his gun belt and dropped it an easy chair in the front room. He lit a kerosene oil lamp which provided a muted glow in the front room, then another coughing fit seized him. He waited until it had passed, then loaded the groceries onto the countertop.

Doc turned on the lamplight and froze.

Waco was sitting on a rocking chair in the front room with his gun lying beside him. "Evenin', Doc," Waco murmured. "Been a long time. Set that lamp down real easy."

Doc set the oil-fired kerosene lamp down on a card table. He remained where he was, just outside the aura of the lamp's glow. The .45 gun in Waco's lap did not move an inch.

"How did you find me?" Doc asked.

"Been tracking you for a while now. Instructions from Blackjack Shackleton. He has a present for Kyle Bascomb. Blackjack will be here directly." Waco glanced around Doc's front room. "So this where you live now? In a ghost town?"

"That's right."

"No one else is here?"

"No one."

"Seems a little creepy to me, but each to his own," Waco said. "How long has it been since you laid eyes on Kyle?"

"Fair time," Doc admitted.

Doc had inched a little closer to the card table where the kerosene lamp was sitting precariously. Waco had not noted the small movement at all. Doc was still shrouded by shadows. Waco nodded, as if that made sense to him.

"Shackleton has a score to settle with the marshal. He has something that belongs to Blackjack and he wants it back. He is willing to do a little horse trading."

The loose shutter outside on Saratoga Street had started banging again in the wind. Waco turned toward it.

Doc took another small step toward to the card table.

Waco looked back at him immediately. Doc's hand had not gone down to the card table. His full attention was focused on the gunman. "What does Blackjack Shackleton have that Marshal Bascomb would want?"

"A hostage."

"What hostage would that be?"

"I believe her name is Abigail, but she answers to the name of 'Skeeter.'"

Doc allowed the shock of that statement to register with him. Then he said: "She is a child," and realized his mistake.

Waco smirked. "Things about kids, they all grow up. Skeeter is a young lady now. I ain't seen her yet, but from what I have heard she's still feisty as all get out."

Doc took one last step toward the card table. "And Shackleton has a gun pointed at her head?"

"Wouldn't surprise me none," Waco sneered.

He heard horses on the streets and half-turned again.

With a lightning move, Doc threw the oil lamp at Waco, the glass funnel smashing. Hot oil splashed up into Waco's face. He screamed. At the same time, Doc kicked over the easy chair. His gun belt dropped onto the floor. Blinded by the kerosene, Waco brought up his gun. Doc grabbed his .45 revolver from the floor and fired. Waco convulsed, but he managed to get to his feet, dragging glass shards from the oil lamp with him. He fired again but missed Doc in the low light. He pulled his Bowie knife from his belt and threw it at Doc. It missed him by an inch. Doc fired again and Waco collapsed back into the rocking chair, dead.

Doc slowly got to his feet. Hot oil and glass fragments were littered across Waco's body. He picked up Waco's Bowie knife and threw it down onto the kitchen counter. He moved into the bedroom, opened the chest of drawers there and brought out the .45 revolver that had been wrapped in cashmere. He brought it onto the patio and unwrapped it. He put the gun belt on and checked that the pearl-handled revolver was loaded. Then he moved out of the house into the raging storm and started to make his way through the back streets of Retribution.

The storm continued to rage over the derelict buildings of Retribution. Kyle Bascomb's figure could be seen in the entrance to the Crystal Palace Saloon. He was ten years older, more rugged, more lines in his face. Two ghostly figures moved in the misty gloom down one of the boardwalks on Saratoga Street. They had their guns drawn. There was one horse tied up outside the Last Chance Saloon. Kyle thought he heard a noise outside in the storm, but the wind seized it and he realized it was a loose shutter banging in the wind.

But he knew they were coming for him.

Kyle moved through the swing doors back into the saloon.

Outside, Doc Holiday moved down a side street, his pearl-handled gun in its holster. He coughed suddenly, turning away, smothering the cough in his handkerchief. It subsided and he moved on.

On Saratoga Street, a rider emerged out of the gloom of the storm. A figure was lying face down across the saddle of his horse. He reached the Crystal Palace Saloon and dismounted. The two lookouts posted in front of the Last Chance Saloon gave them the "all clear" signal. The rider pulled a figure from over the saddle and manhandled the prisoner toward the swing doors of the saloon.

Doc came up behind one of the two outlaw lookouts and coldcocked him. He dragged him from the boardwalk and deposited him in a side street.

Blackjack Shackleton entered the Crystal Palace Saloon. Kyle Bascomb stayed where he was at one of the tables, sipping his whiskey. He noted that the years had not been kind to Shackleton. His face was drawn and scarred. He threw his prisoner to the floor of the saloon.

It was *Skeeter*.

She had matured into a young woman of twenty-four-years now. She had the same, instantly recognizable face that Marshal Bascomb remembered. She was wearing a Lea Floral-print silk-satin Jacquard midi dress. She was rebellious and as ebullient as ever. But she was also very frightened. She got shakily to her feet. Her hands were tied with rawhide ropes. She looked over at Kyle.

"Morning, Marshal," she said. "It has been a long time since I last saw you."

"Has," Kyle said.

Skeeter glared at Blackjack Shackleton. "He grabbed me right off the street in Denver," she said, defiantly. "I did not recognize the bastard at first. But you do not forget the face of the man who killed your father."

When Shackleton spoke his words, there was a rasp to them. "As I recall, Skeeter, your daddy was shooting at me at the time."

Kyle looked over. "You doin' okay, Skeeter?"

"I am fine, Marshal, she said, rebelliously.

Blackjack looked at Kyle, as if ironic. "No back up, Marshal?"

"Your telegram said to come alone," Kyle said. "You watched me ride in. There was no one with me. And I'm not a marshal anymore."

"Just a concerned citizen with the life of a young girl in your hands."

Kyle just waited, his hands on the table, palms down, watching Blackjack.

Paul Taggart moved down the street outside the Crystal Palace Saloon. He drew his gun out of its holster. The years also had taken a toll on him as well as Blackjack Shackleton. He climbed the staircase in the alleyway to-ward the wide balcony on the second floor.

Doc stepped out into the open. The second gunman on the streets of Retribution whirled on him. Doc drew first and shot him dead. A crack of thunder obliterated the sound of the gunshot. Doc dragged the man's body into the alleyway. Across the street, Taggart reached the balcony of the Crystal Palace Saloon. He accessed one of the French doors that let him into the building,

Doc ran through the downpour to the staircase and climbed up after Paul Taggart. Three of the stairs were missing. Doc had to pull himself up onto Deke's balcony. A coughing fit wracked him. He stifled it, took a moment to get his breath back, then followed Taggart onto the second floor.

Inside the Crystal Palace Saloon, Kyle still faced Blackjack Shackleton. A look from Kyle had stopped Skeeter from moving. He said conversationally: "Still robbing trains and banks, Blackjack?"

Shackleton shook his head. "Time's change. Civilization's crowdin' in. Spent some time in Mexico with Juarez and his revolutionaries."

Kyle was ironic. "Nice to be fighting for a cause."

Shackleton looked out the swing doors down the main street of Retribution.

"A lot of towns ended up like this," he said. "I hear cholera swept through Retribution like a prairie fire. One by one all of the businesses failed and got boarded up. People left. What happened to your lady doctor friend? What was her name again? Rachel, that was it."

"I don't rightly know," Kyle said.

"You let that filly slip through your fingers?"

"I did."

"She took care of me when I was at death's door. A fine lady."

"Cut Skeeter's ropes," Kyle said.

Shackleton turned back to him. "First we have unsettled business to attend to."

"What would that be?"

"My pocket watch," Blackjack said, softly.

"What made you come back for it after all these years?"

"Waco saw you on the street of Abilene a month back. He was still working occasionally for me as a gun hand. I knew that Retribution had now become a ghost town. Seemed the fitting place for us to have a rendezvous. That pocket watch has a sentimental attachment for me, Marshal. Never thought I would see it again. But here we are."

"And you kidnapped Abigail as a hostage?"

"I knew you were kindly disposed to her. I will let her go just as soon as we have concluded our business."

Kyle reached into the pocket of his slicker and set the ornate pocket watch on the table beside his rifle. Shackleton stared down at it for a moment in the shadows of the saloon. He shook his head.

"That could be a fancy timepiece you picked up in your wanderin's."

"The initials on the pocket watch are '*J.S.*'"

Kyle flipped it open. Outside the storm raged, thunder echoed, but inside the saloon it was as if a hush had come over the place. The pocket watch played its distinctive *Greensleeves* tune.

Above them, at the back of the saloon, Paul Taggart moved forward down the corridor, gun in hand. Doc emerged onto the second-floor landing from what had once been Deke Reneker's room. Ahead of him, he saw Taggart moving closer to the staircase.

Below them, Kyle said: "Let your hostage go now."

Shackleton took out a knife and cut the bonds binding Skeeter. She massaged her wrists. Shackleton grabbed hold of her shoulders, holding her tight. Kyle had still not moved his position in the chair.

"I nudge her over to the table," Shackleton said. "You throw me the pocket watch."

Skeeter shook her head violently. "He means to kill you, Marshal! There are others with him!"

"I brought back-up," Shackleton admitted. "You knew I would do that. But there is no one in here but us, Marshal. Simple exchange."

Kyle's eyes flickered to the mirror over the bar. In reflection he saw Paul Taggart reach the top of the stairs. He looked back at Blackjack Shackleton.

"Your call," he said.

Shackleton pushed Skeeter hard over to Kyle. Kyle threw Shackleton the pocket watch and hit the floor, grabbing his rifle. Above him Taggart fired. Taggart's bullets splintered the table. Shackleton drew his gun. On the floor, Kyle fired the rifle, blowing Shackleton back through the swing doors.

Taggart had Kyle cold, aiming at his head.

Doc came down the second-floor staircase firing. Taggart whirled, got off two shots, then fell under a hail of bullets from Doc's Colt .45 revolver. He plunged down the staircase and lay at the bottom. Kyle acknowledged Doc as he knelt beside Shackleton's body. Doc holstered his gun and came the rest of the way down the staircase.

Skeeter looked at Doc Holliday with a big grin on her face. "That pearl-handled revolver still looks great on you!"

Doc glanced at Kyle who had dragged Shackleton's dead body back inside the saloon.

"I only wear it when I'm with Kyle," he said, dryly.

Abigail was excited. "You came all the way back to Retribution to rescue me! Wow! Shit!"

"Language, Skeeter," Doc said, automatically. "Though I guess you're old enough now to talk any way you please. What name do you answer to these days?"

"Abigail, but you can always call me Skeeter."

"I guess Doc didn't actually have to travel very far to back me up," Kyle said.

"I still live in Retribution," Doc said.

Skeeter looked at both of them in amazement.

The storm had blown itself out but had left dark clouds threatening to drench the town again. Distant thunder echoed almost eerily through the deserted streets of Retribution. Skeeter was on the patio of Doc Holliday's cottage admiring the painting of the girl whom she believed might be Doc's daughter up on the easel. Kyle stood near the door with Doc, who was putting on a dry silk shirt.

"I figured Shackleton would bring men with him," Kyle said. "But how did Waco get here?"

"He saw me in Kettleberg. I get into town every few days to load up with provisions. Waco followed me to Retribution. He had been going to meet up with Blackjack when he brought Skeeter back here. It was pure chance that Waco and I ran into each other."

"The assistance was much appreciated." Kyle said.

Skeeter turned from the painting, looking at Doc. "I heard you had died of consumption at the Glenwood Springs in Colorado ten years ago," she said. "I bawled my eyes out."

Doc said: "A prematurely gray-haired and ailing young man, of my approximate age, did pass on into the arms of eternity on November 9th, 1887. He was buried as Doctor John Henry Holliday. It was his moment of infamy."

"When did you come back to Retribution?" Skeeter wanted to know.

"Roughly eight years ago."

"What brought to a ghost town?" Kyle asked.

"To die, as I thought," Doc said, "but the Grim Reaper appeared reluctant to claim the soul of a gunfighter and a rather poor dentist. I have been living here ever since."

Skeeter looked back at the painting of Doc's daughter. "I told you you'd finish it. She is beautiful. I am sorry she never got to grow up."

Doc shrugged. "At least I had a surrogate daughter for a spell."

Skeeter's smile lit up the room. "Do you mean that?"

"I will allow some credence to that statement."

"I'll take the bodies into Tombstone," Kyle said, "and contact the marshal there."

"Is there a reward for Blackjack Shackleton and his gang?" Doc asked.

"Might be."

"I'd appreciate it if you would tell the marshal in Tombstone that *you* wiped out what was left of the Shackleton gang singlehanded. I would like the word of my untimely demise to go unchallenged."

Skeeter looked around the patio, shaking her head. "How can you survive in a *ghost town*, Doc? It has got to be lonely for you."

"I find my own company preferable to the dead souls who inhabit the town."

Kyle turned to Skeeter. "Have you kept in touch with Homer over these years?"

"Oh, I married him," Skeeter said. "The ruffian rat is in Washington right now. Going to run for Congress."

Kyle opened the patio door and noted that the storm was again threatening. "We need to go."

"One minute," Doc said.

He disappeared into the front room and returned with the small painting of the *Retribution Sunset*. He wrapped a cloth around it and handed it to Skeeter.

"So you won't forget," he said.

Skeeter looked as if Doc had just given her the most wonderful Christmas present. She hugged him.

"I could never forget you, Doc," she said, softly.

"I will allow some truth to that," he said.

Out in Retribution, sunshine filtered through the clouds. In front of the Crystal Palace Saloon, Kyle had draped the five outlaw bodies over the saddles of three horses. Skeeter would ride the fourth horse.

Skeeter took Doc's hands in hers. There was a different dynamic between them. Tender, but adult. "Maybe one day Homer and I will come back to Retribution and visit you," she said.

"Don't wait too long," Doc told her. "I thought I might go up to the Yukon Territories. I hear it is beautiful up there. Could be beneficial for my cough."

"Will you miss me just a little?" she asked him.

"I will give it some thought," Doc said, softly. "Goodbye, Abigail."

This time Skeeter kissed Doc lightly on the lips. "Goodbye, Doc."

She climbed up onto the horse. Doc glanced at Kyle. "Kettleberg is not far from Retribution," he said, casually. "Might be worthwhile for you to take a trip there."

"It might be at that," Kyle said. He took a yellowed newspaper out of his saddlebag and handed it to Doc. "Wyatt Earp wrote this about ya."

Doc opened the newspaper clipping. He read: "Doc

was a dentist, not a lawman or an assassin; whom necessity had made a gambler; a gentleman whom disease had made a frontier vagabond; a philosopher whom life had made a caustic wit." He read further on: "He was deadliest man with a six-gun."

Tears suddenly filled Doc's diseased eyes. He just nodded.

"Wyatt allowed that you were a loyal friend and good company," Kyle said.

"He always did allow sentiment to color his reflections," Doc murmured.

"Should I let him know…" Kyle began.

"Let him believe I took in the vapors in that sanitarium like he'd always wanted me to," Doc said, "and that I succumbed there. The arms of morbius will be reaching for me soon enough."

Doc pocketed the newspaper article in his vest pocket. Above them, Skeeter said: "I never did find out which one of you would pull leather faster."

Kyle and Doc looked at each another. Both of them pulled leather. Doc's gun was out of his holster just a whisker before Kyle's. Skeeter whistled. Her eyes were shining.

"I knew it! I knew you would be faster, Doc!"

Kyle and Doc shook hands. Doc said, sotto voce: "You slowed up."

Kyle murmured: "Every kid needs a hero. Even if it *is* Doc Holliday."

Kyle mounted his horse. He and Skeeter rode past the Crystal Palace Saloon, the other horses trailing behind. Doc Holliday walked down the main street of Retribution toward his cottage, but this time the ghosts did not haunt him.

Kyle waited for her in front of a stone house with blue trim on the shutters. She had just come down a flagstone path. For a moment she could not move. Her breath tangled up in her throat. He smiled at her, as if he had been waiting for her to arrive at that very moment all his life. Then she burst into tears and ran to him. Rachel threw her arms around Kyle and kissed him is if she would lose him forever.

They stayed that way for a very long time.

Doc Holliday stepped off the stagecoach in the Yukon Territories in a town called Forty Mile. It was a hardscrabble, sprawling frontier town surrounded by white-capped mountains. Doc took a breath of the cold, clear air. The raucous ambiance of the town permeated his soul and he knew that this was a place he would find rewarding.

He might even find a poker game being played in the local saloon.

As long at the inhabitants of Forty Mile did not find out that he was the legendary Doc Holliday.

THE END

www.ingramcontent.com/pod-product-compliance
Lightning Source LLC
Chambersburg PA
CBHW051837020726
47502CB00005B/1825